BAD KITTY

Meets the BABY

NICK BRUEL

SQUARE FISH

ROARING BROOK PRESS
New York

For Emma, Isaac,
Lila, Will,
and Isabel

SQUARE
FISH

An Imprint of Macmillan

Square Fish and the Square Fish logo are trademarks of Macmillan and
are used by Roaring Brook Press under license from Macmillan.

Library of Congress Cataloging-in-Publication Data

Bruel, Nick.
    Bad kitty meets the baby / Nick Bruel.
        p. cm.
    "A Neal Porter Book."
    Summary: Bad kitty is not pleased when a baby joins her family. Includes
fun facts and tips for training a cat to perform tricks.
    ISBN 978-0-312-64121-4
    [1. Cats—Fiction. 2. Babies—Fiction. 3. Adoption—Fiction. 4. Humorous
stories.] I. Title.
    PZ7.B82832Bam 2011
    [E]—dc22

                                                        2010035699

Originally published in the United States by Roaring Brook Press
First Square Fish Edition: January 2012
Square Fish logo designed by Filomena Tuosto
mackids.com

17   19   20   18

AR: 3.6 / LEXILE: 720L

• CONTENTS •

•INTRODUCTION•
IN THE BEGINNING

IN THE BEGINNING, THERE WAS KITTY.

Just Kitty.

Only Kitty.

Kitty—all by herself.

And life was good.

Kitty ate her food—alone.

Kitty played with her toys—alone.

Kitty slept on the sofa—alone.

The years passed, and Kitty was happy to eat alone, play alone, and sleep alone. Life continued to be good—alone.

BUT ONE DAY . . .

. . . the skies became dark, the ground began to shake, the air became cold and dank and filled with a horrible stench.

8

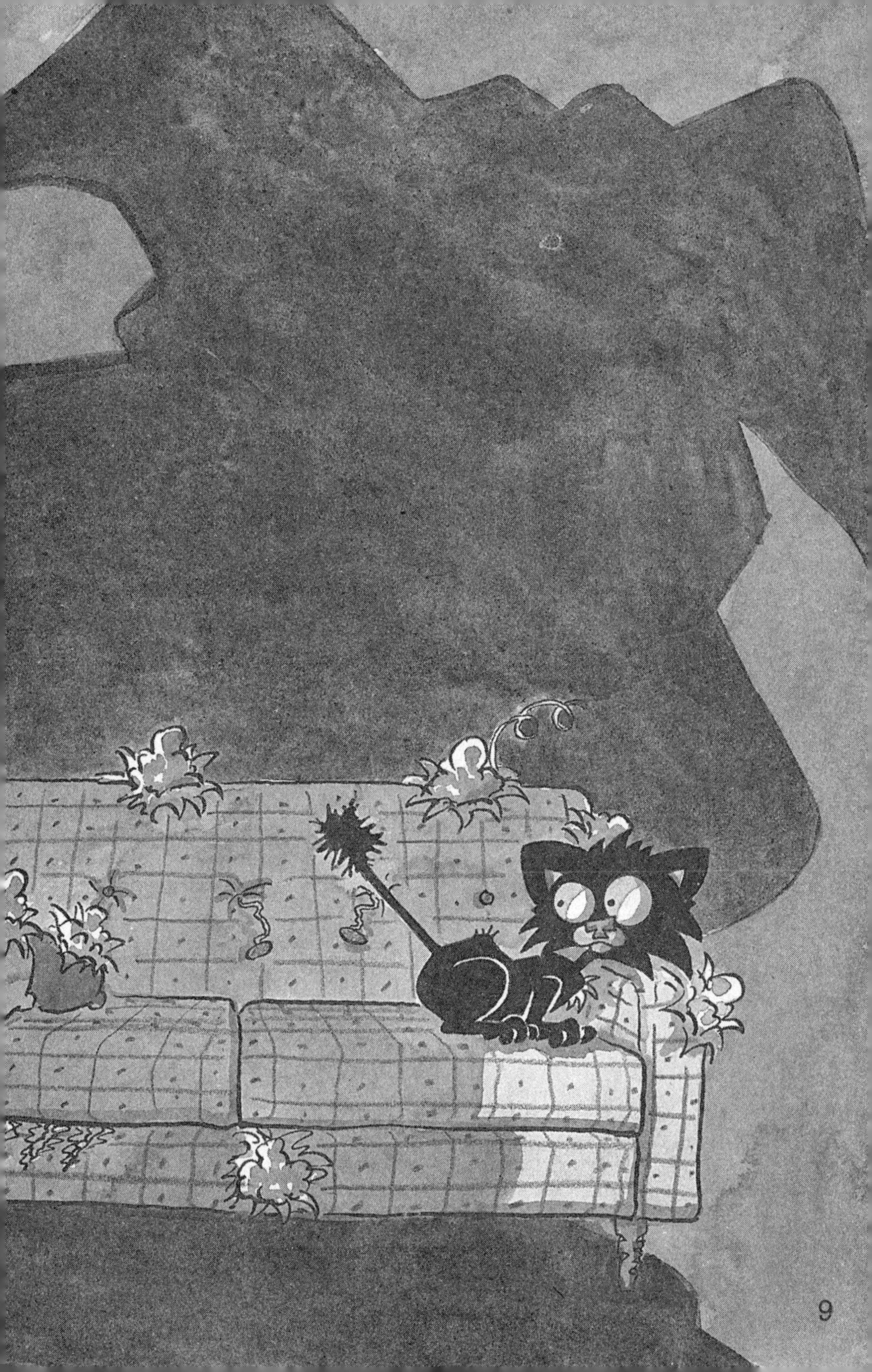

A foul and wretched beast had arrived as if from nowhere.

Its face was deformed and grotesque. Its massive black nose was always cold and always wet. Its breath was so hot and so foul that its odor could mask the stench of a hundred dead fish lying in the sun. And it seemed to be filled with a noxious, clear liquid that continuously dripped out of the vast, gaping maw it called its mouth.

But what was worst of all, worse than its ugliness, worse than its terrible stink, and even worse than the never-ending trail of ooze it left behind wherever it went . . .

. . . was that the beast never seemed to sleep.

Kitty fought bravely to rid her once peaceful kingdom of the cruel beast. But even she wasn't mighty enough to defeat the evil creature.

Every time they confronted each other, the hideous beast would smear his foul, oily liquid on Kitty as if preparing to devour her.

Survival became a daily challenge for poor Kitty.

Over time, Kitty became used to life with the beast. Even its horrible odor became tolerable. The brave Kitty had found areas of shelter where she could evade the beast and its terrible liquid.

At times, though she would never admit it, she became almost fond of the beast.

Almost.

Life was not as it once was, but eventually it became good again.

Little did Kitty know that soon there would be another.

•CHAPTER ONE•

A SHORT TIME AWAY

GOOD MORNING, KITTY!

I suppose you're wondering why there are so many bags and suitcases on the floor.

Well, that's because we're going on a very special trip!

Uh . . . that is . . . WE are going on a very special trip. Sorry, Kitty, but you'll be staying here at home with Puppy.

Oh, don't be like that, Kitty. We won't be gone for long. And when we get back from our very special trip, we'll have a very special surprise for you.

Meanwhile, good ol' Uncle Murray has agreed to stay here and take good care of you and Puppy while we're away. Isn't that nice?

Hi, dog. Hi there, ya goofy cat. We're going to have some fun together. Right?

So, Kitty, make sure that you listen to everything that Uncle Murray tells you. And make sure that you play nicely with Puppy. And make sure that you don't make a big mess while we're away.

Ahhh . . . We're going to get along just fine! Right, cat?!

Goodbye, Kitty! Goodbye, Puppy! Goodbye, Uncle Murray! We'll see you in one week!

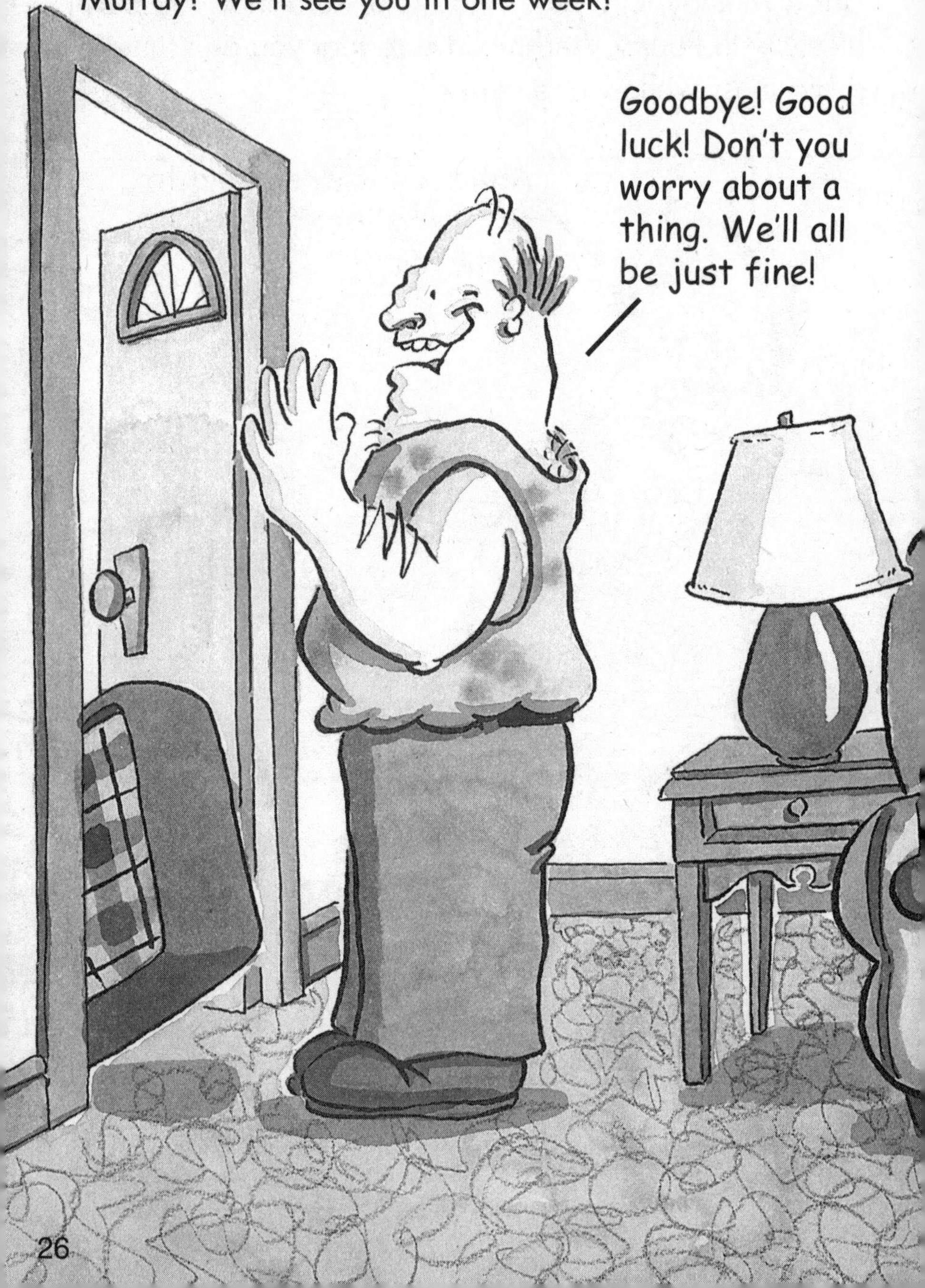
Goodbye! Good luck! Don't you worry about a thing. We'll all be just fine!

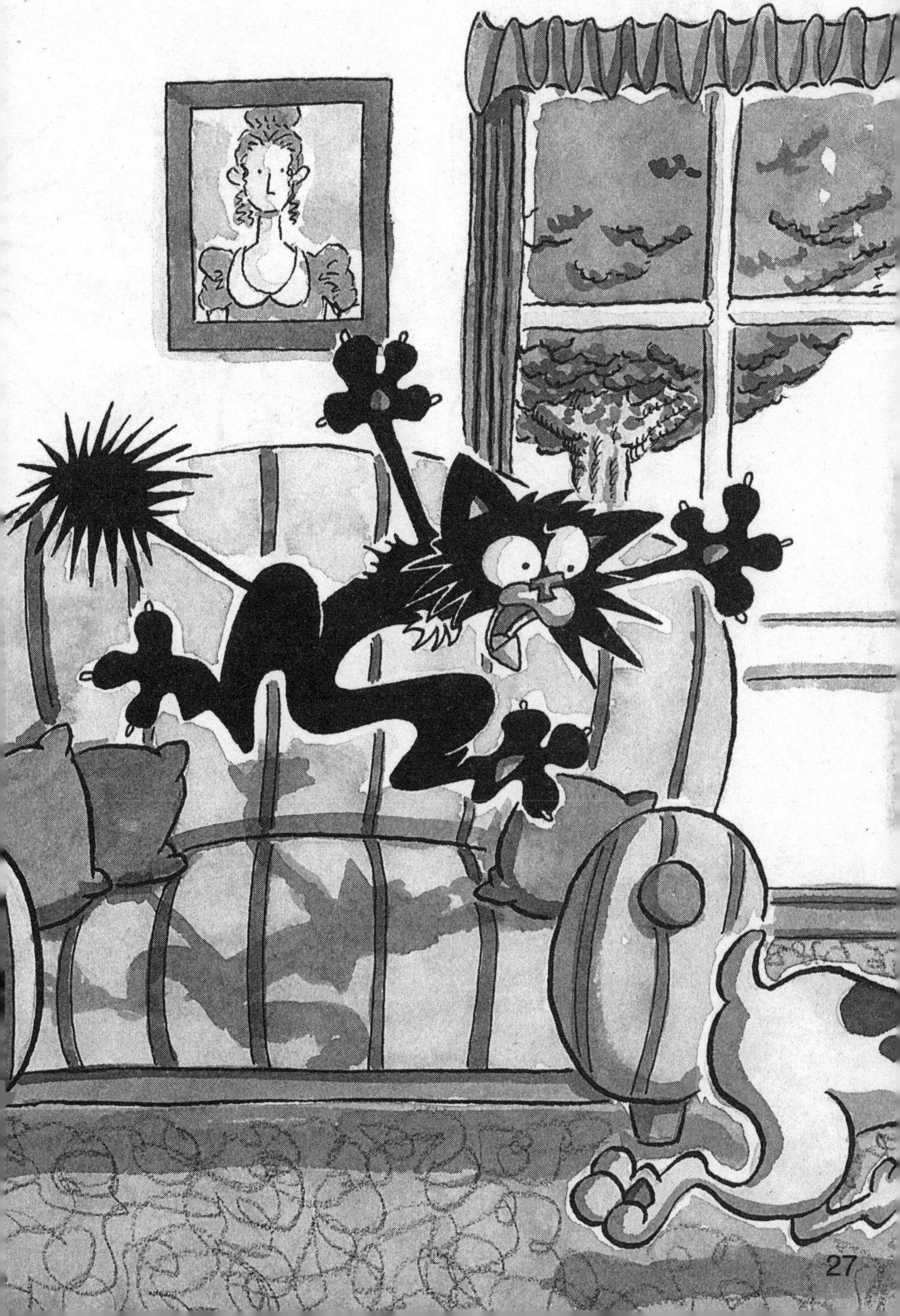

DAY ONE

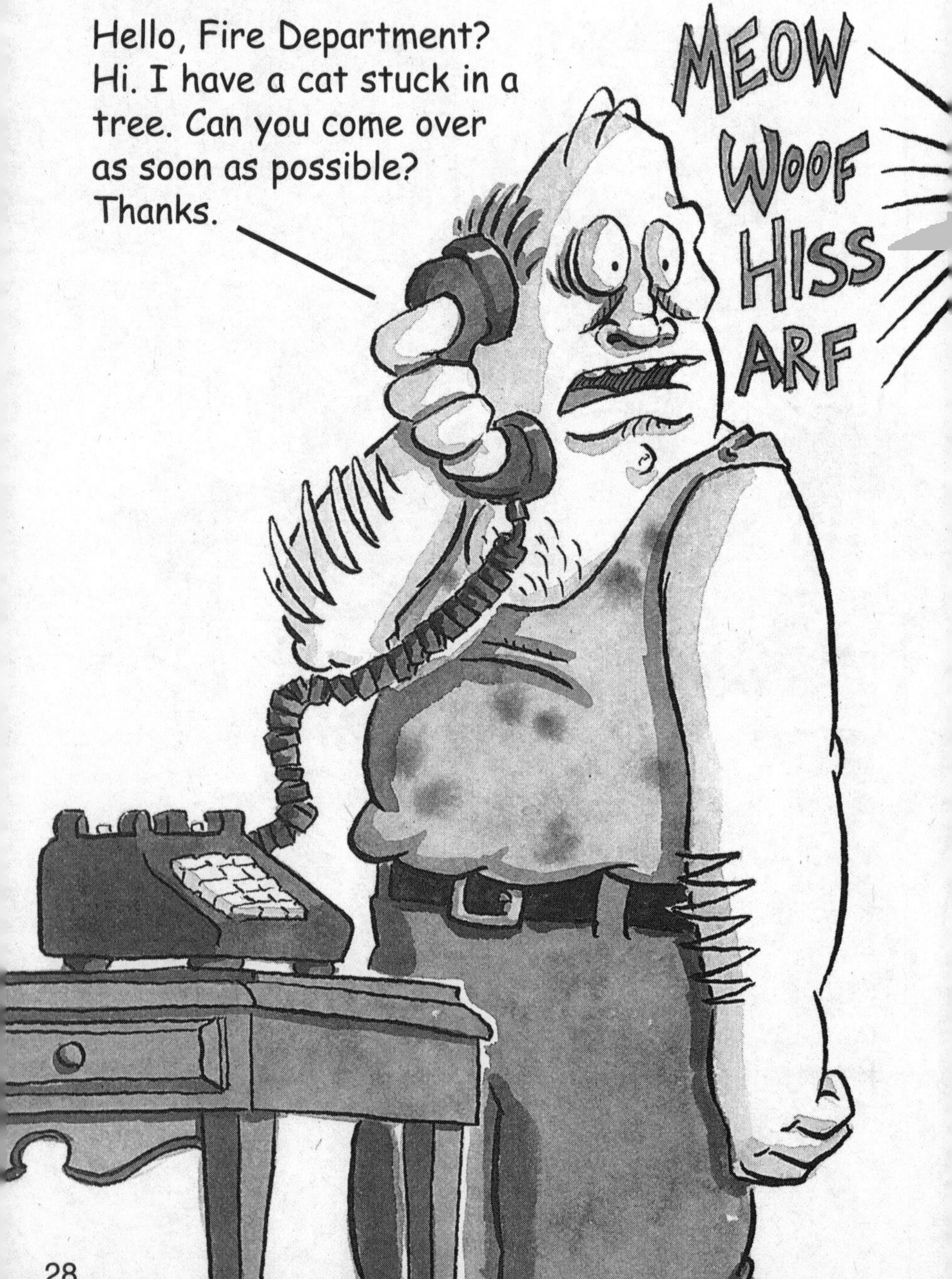
Hello, Fire Department? Hi. I have a cat stuck in a tree. Can you come over as soon as possible? Thanks.
MEOW
WOOF
HISS
ARF

DAY TWO

Hello, Fire Department? Hi. I have a dog stuck in a tree. That's right. I said "dog." Can you come right over? Thanks!

DAY THREE

Hello, Fire Department? Hi. It's me again. Heh-heh! Well, you're not going to believe this, but that cat and dog are both stuck up in that tree again and . . . you know the address. Thank you.

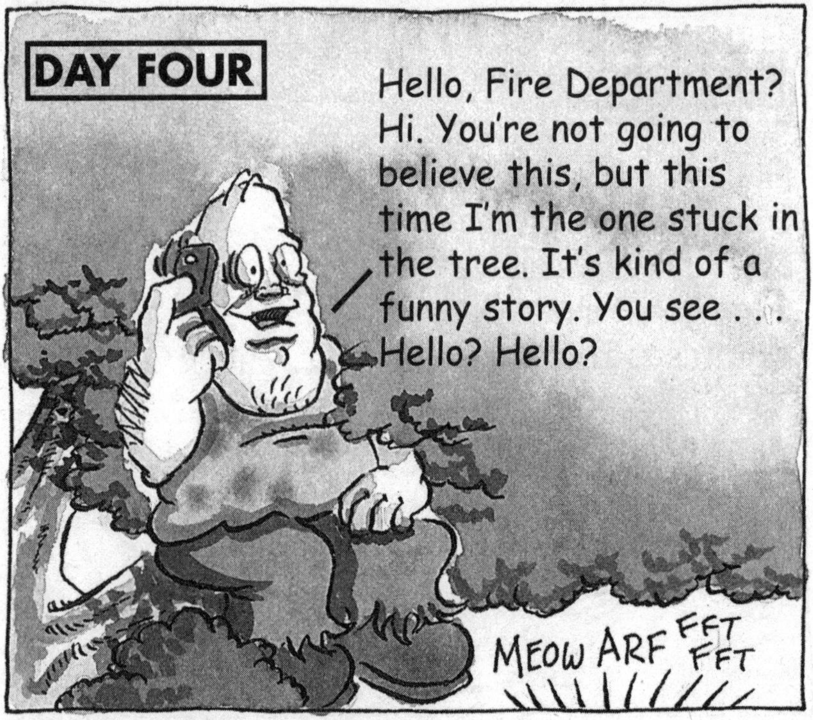
DAY FOUR
Hello, Fire Department? Hi. You're not going to believe this, but this time I'm the one stuck in the tree. It's kind of a funny story. You see . . . Hello? Hello?
MEOW ARF FFT FFT

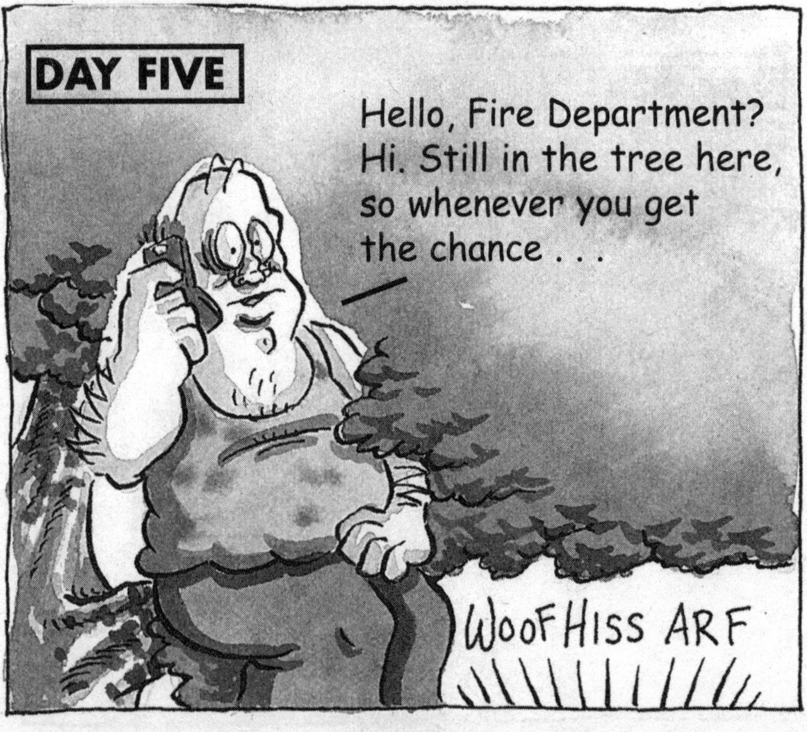
DAY FIVE
Hello, Fire Department? Hi. Still in the tree here, so whenever you get the chance . . .
WOOF HISS ARF

UNCLE MURRAY'S FUN FACTS

WHY DO CATS CLIMB TREES?

'Cause they're out of their #@% minds! That's why!

All cats like to climb trees. Even big cats like lions and jaguars (but not most tigers) like to climb trees. And they all do it for three different reasons.

1)  Cats like to climb trees . . . well . . . because they like to. Cats aren't very tall, so climbing up things like trees will give them the opportunity to see their surroundings from up high. Plus, while they're at it, climbing up a tree gives cats the opportunity to sharpen their claws, which they do all the time anyway.

And the higher up they go, the thinner the air, which is why they go #%&*@ crazy!

2)  Cats will also climb trees because they're predators, which means that they hunt other animals. When they climb up a tree to inspect their surroundings, part of what they're looking for is something to eat. And as an added bonus, there happen to be some tasty things like birds and squirrels already nesting in those trees.

 Squirrels?! They eat squirrels?! Birds I knew about. But squirrels?! That's proof that cats are #%&*@ crazy!

3)  Cats may be predators, but there are other bigger animals like dogs who sometimes attack cats. Climbing up a tree can often save a cat from harm.

Don't you believe it! That dog wouldn't hurt a fly!

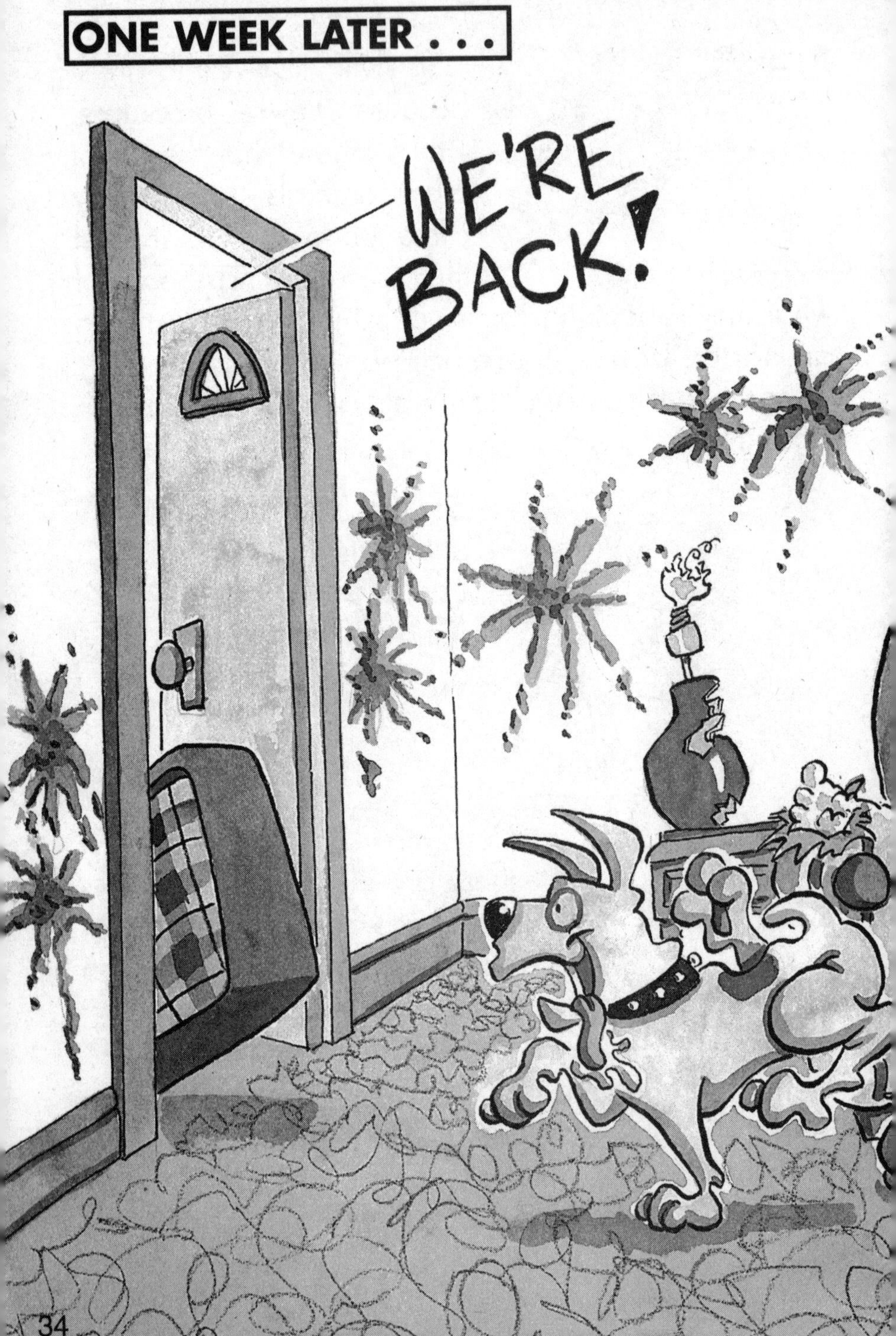
ONE WEEK LATER . . .
WE'RE BACK!

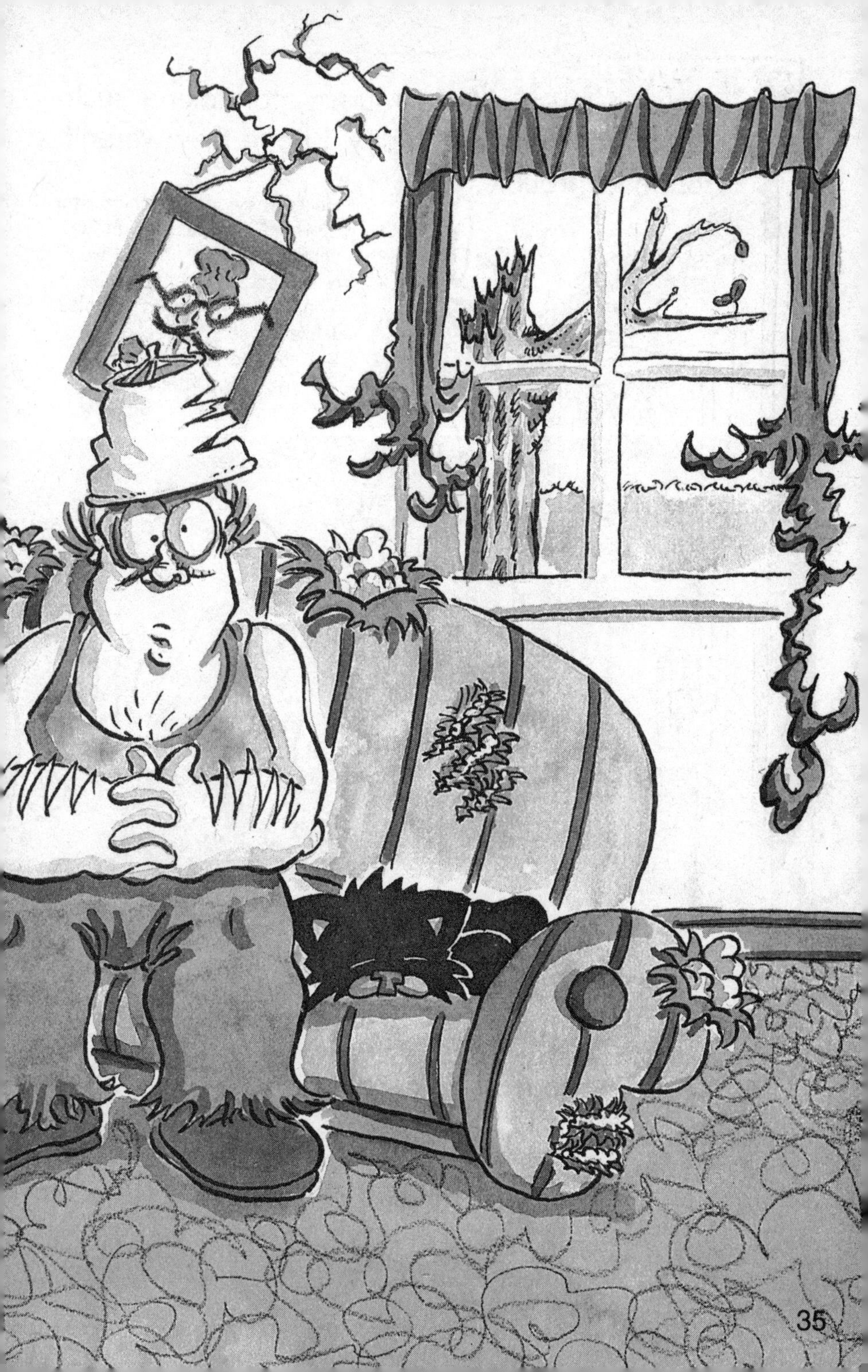

Thank you so much, Uncle Murray, for taking such good care of Kitty and Puppy. I hope they weren't too much trouble.

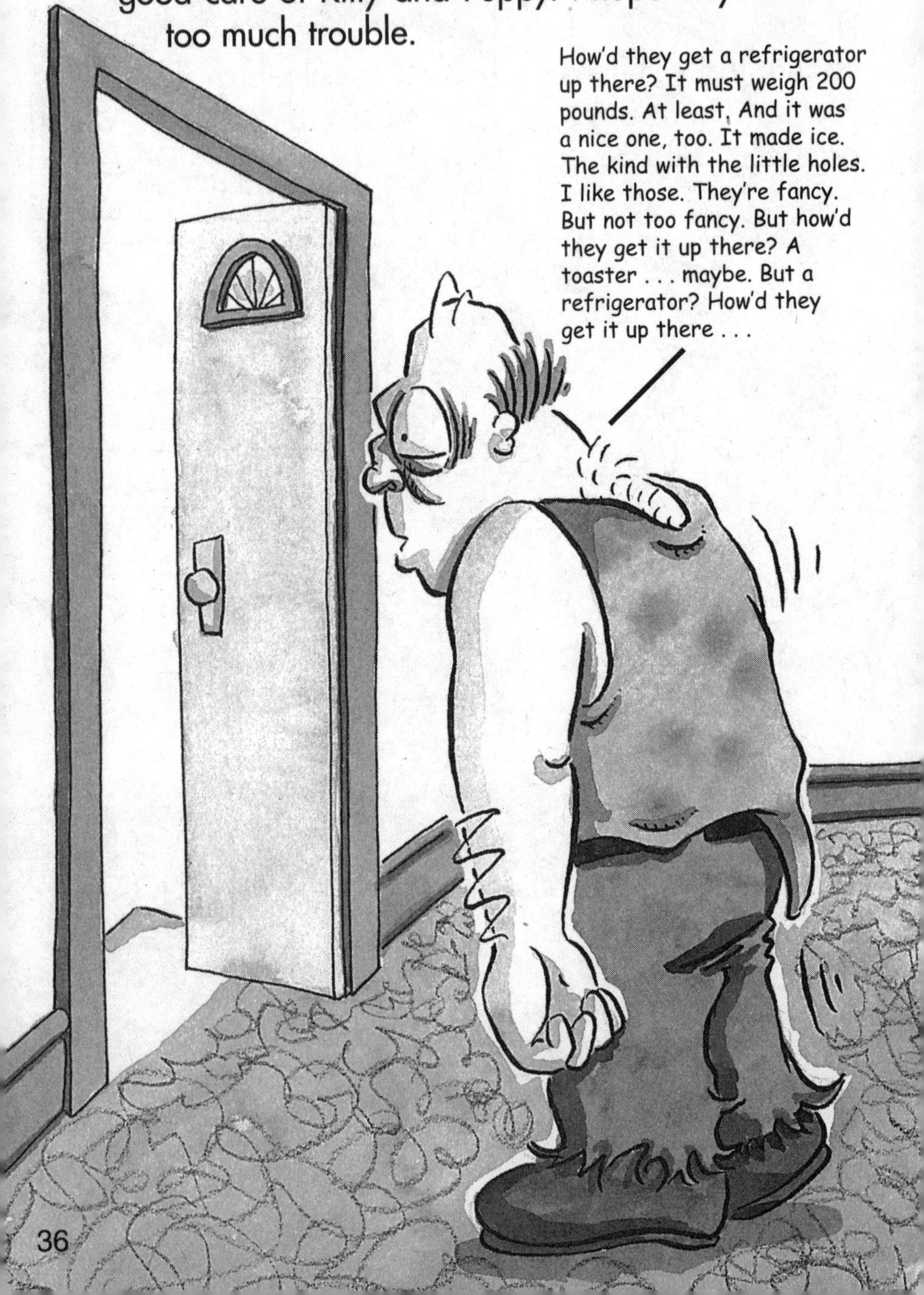
How'd they get a refrigerator up there? It must weigh 200 pounds. At least. And it was a nice one, too. It made ice. The kind with the little holes. I like those. They're fancy. But not too fancy. But how'd they get it up there? A toaster . . . maybe. But a refrigerator? How'd they get it up there . . .

Goodbye, Uncle Murray!

Hi, Kitty. Awww . . . You're not still sore at us for going on that trip without you, are you? Well, this will cheer you up! Do you remember that real big surprise we promised you? Do you? Do you?

WELL, HERE SHE IS!

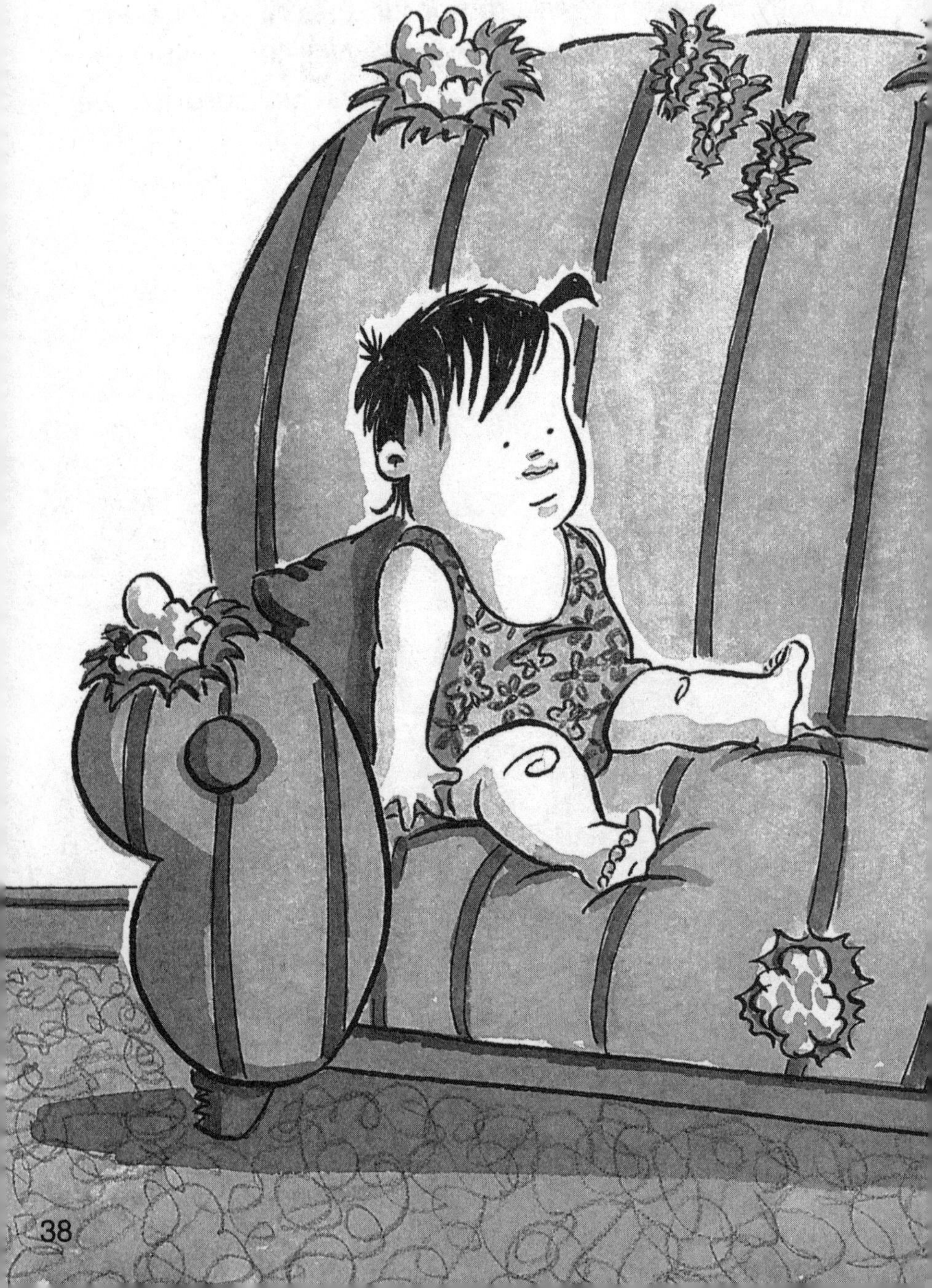

WHAT THE HECK IS THAT THING?

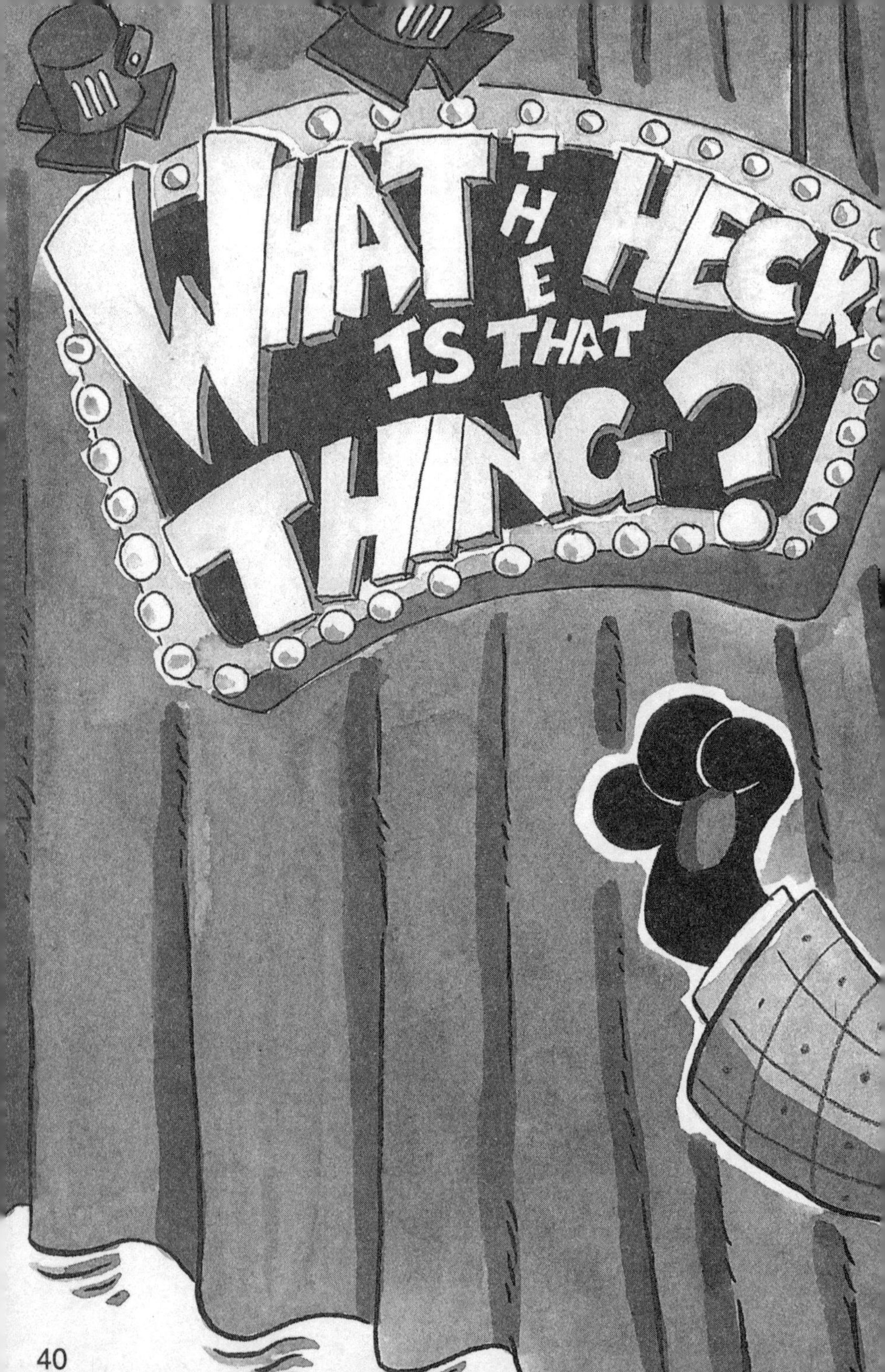
WHAT THE HECK IS THAT THING?

HI THERE! AND WELCOME TO THE INSIDE OF KITTY'S BRAIN AND THE HOTTEST GAME SHOW IN TOWN . . .
WHAT THE HECK IS THAT THING?
?
?

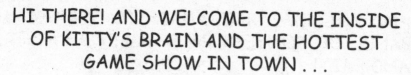

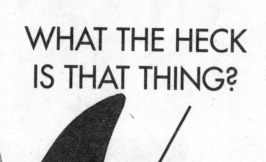

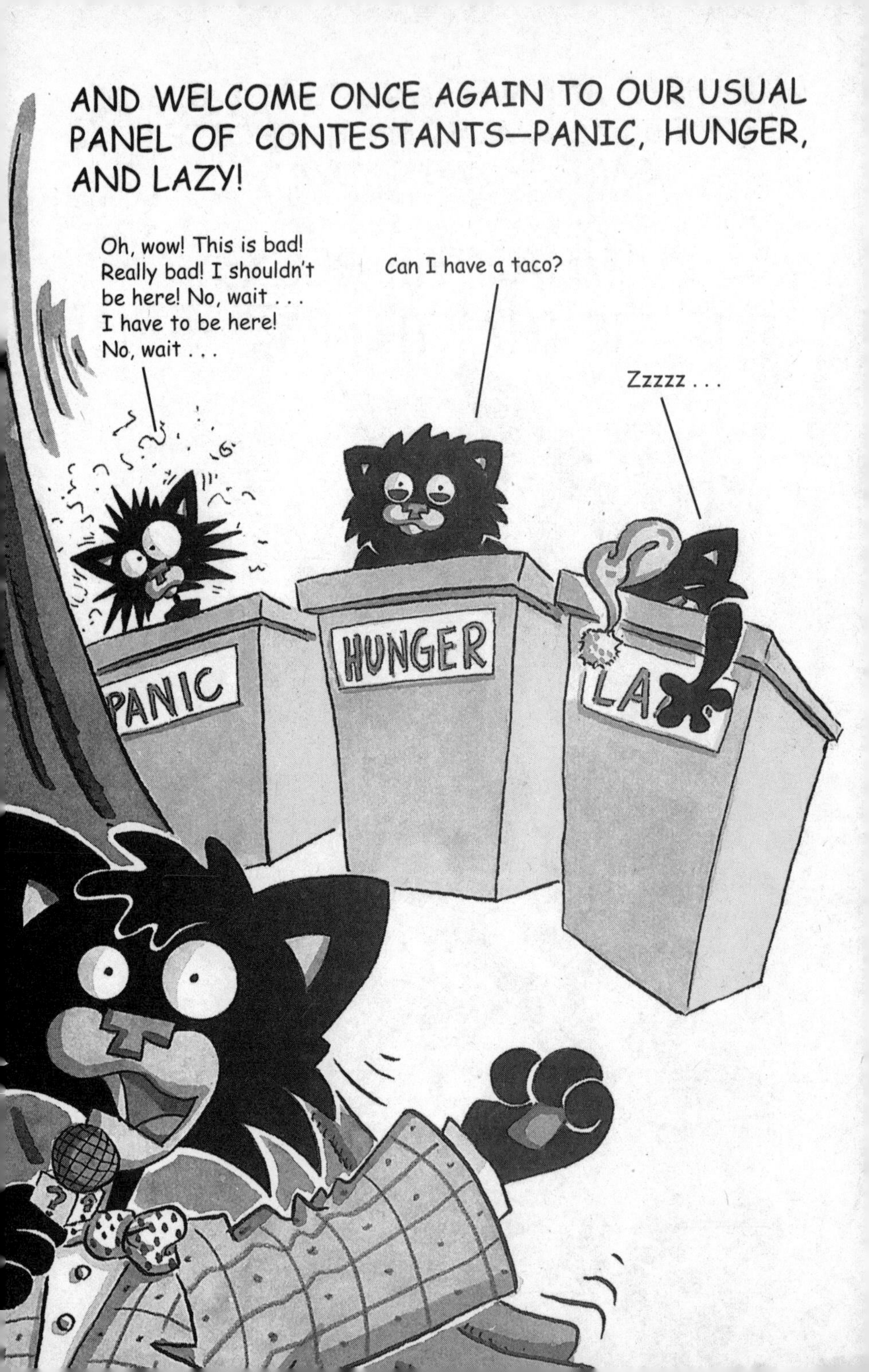
AND WELCOME ONCE AGAIN TO OUR USUAL PANEL OF CONTESTANTS—PANIC, HUNGER, AND LAZY!
Oh, wow! This is bad! Really bad! I shouldn't be here! No, wait . . . I have to be here! No, wait . . .
Can I have a taco?
Zzzzz . . .
PANIC
HUNGER
LA

PANIC, SINCE YOU CAME CLOSEST LAST WEEK WHEN YOU IDENTIFIED THE DUST BALL WE SAW UNDER THE SOFA AS "SOME SORT OF FUZZY COCKROACH MONSTER THAT WILL EAT US ALL," YOU GET TO BE THE FIRST TO PLAY **WHAT THE HECK IS THAT THING?**

Oh, wow! It's big. I mean, it's really big! And it drools a lot! I've never seen anything like it before! I should attack it. No, wait . . . I should run away! No, wait . . . I should attack it! No, wait . . .

HUNGER, IT'S YOUR TURN TO PLAY **WHAT THE HECK IS THAT THING?**

I don't know, but it smells funny . . . like a liver, fish, and onion taco.

LAZY! LET'S HEAR WHAT YOU HAVE TO SAY!
WHAT THE HECK IS THAT THING?

GOOD POINTS, EVERYBODY! IT'S BIG, IT DROOLS, IT SMELLS FUNNY, AND IT'S VERY NOISY! WHAT DO YOU SAY TO THAT, PANIC? ANY GUESSES?

Oh, wow! That's not good! Very bad! Very, very bad! We should attack! No, wait . . . We should run away! No, wait . . .

HUNGER! WHAT SAY YOU, MY FRIEND?

I love milk. I love tuna. I love tacos. But if I mix them all together, I get nauseous. But it's always worth it.

ANYTHING MORE TO ADD, LAZY?

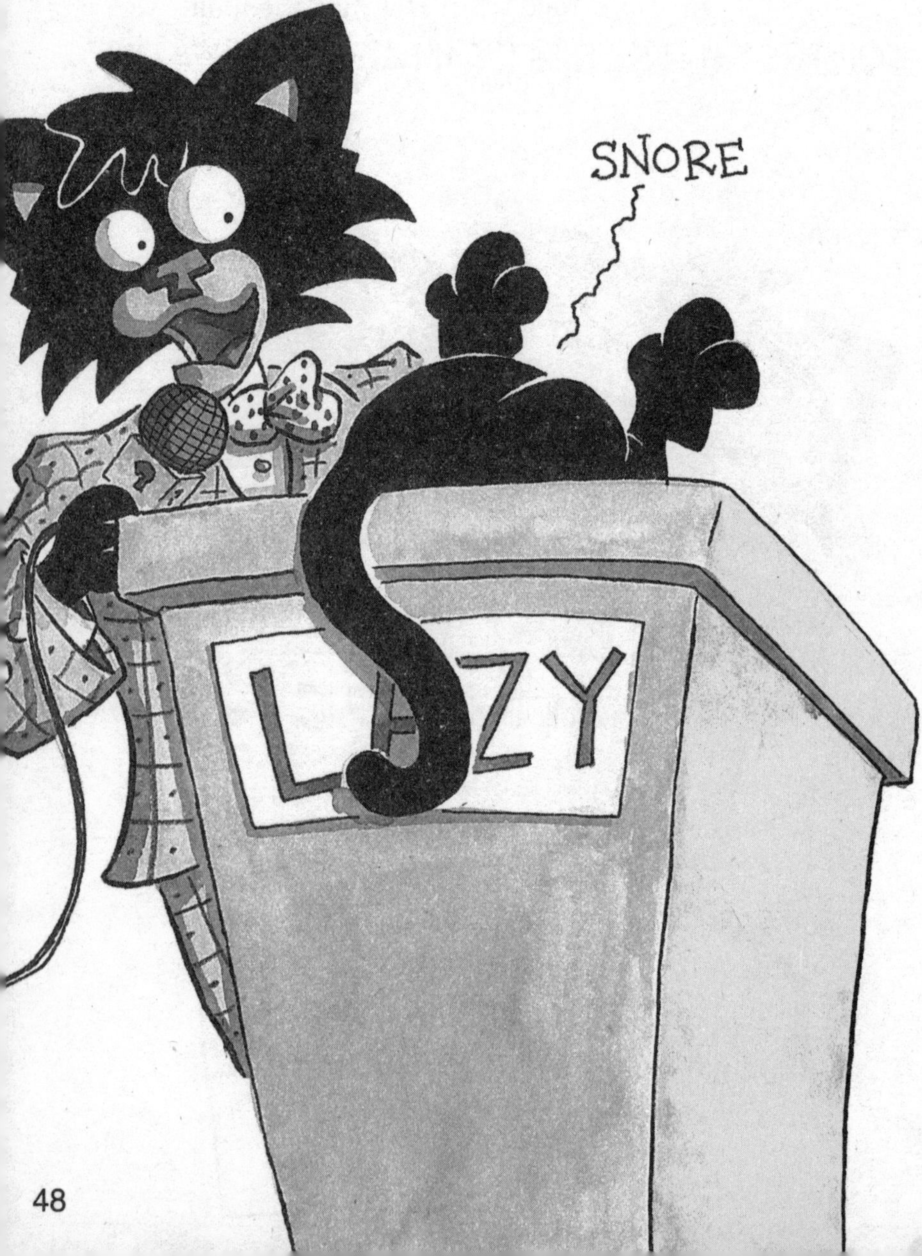
SNORE
LAZY

TIME'S UP, CONTESTANTS! IT'S TIME TO LOCK IN YOUR ANSWERS. REMEMBER . . . THE CLUES ARE: IT'S BIG, IT DROOLS A LOT, IT SMELLS TERRIBLE, AND IT'S NOISY.

CONTESTANTS, THAT CAN MEAN ONLY ONE THING! IT'S . . .

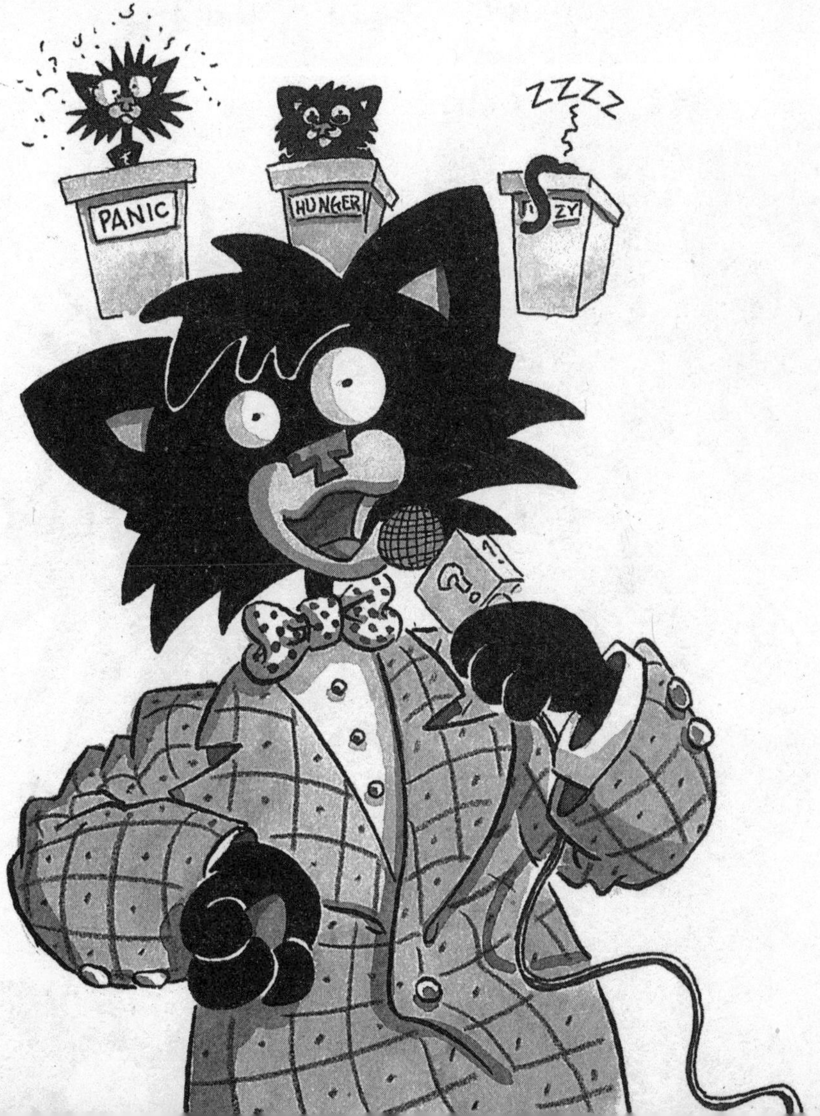

ZZZZ
PANIC
HUNGER

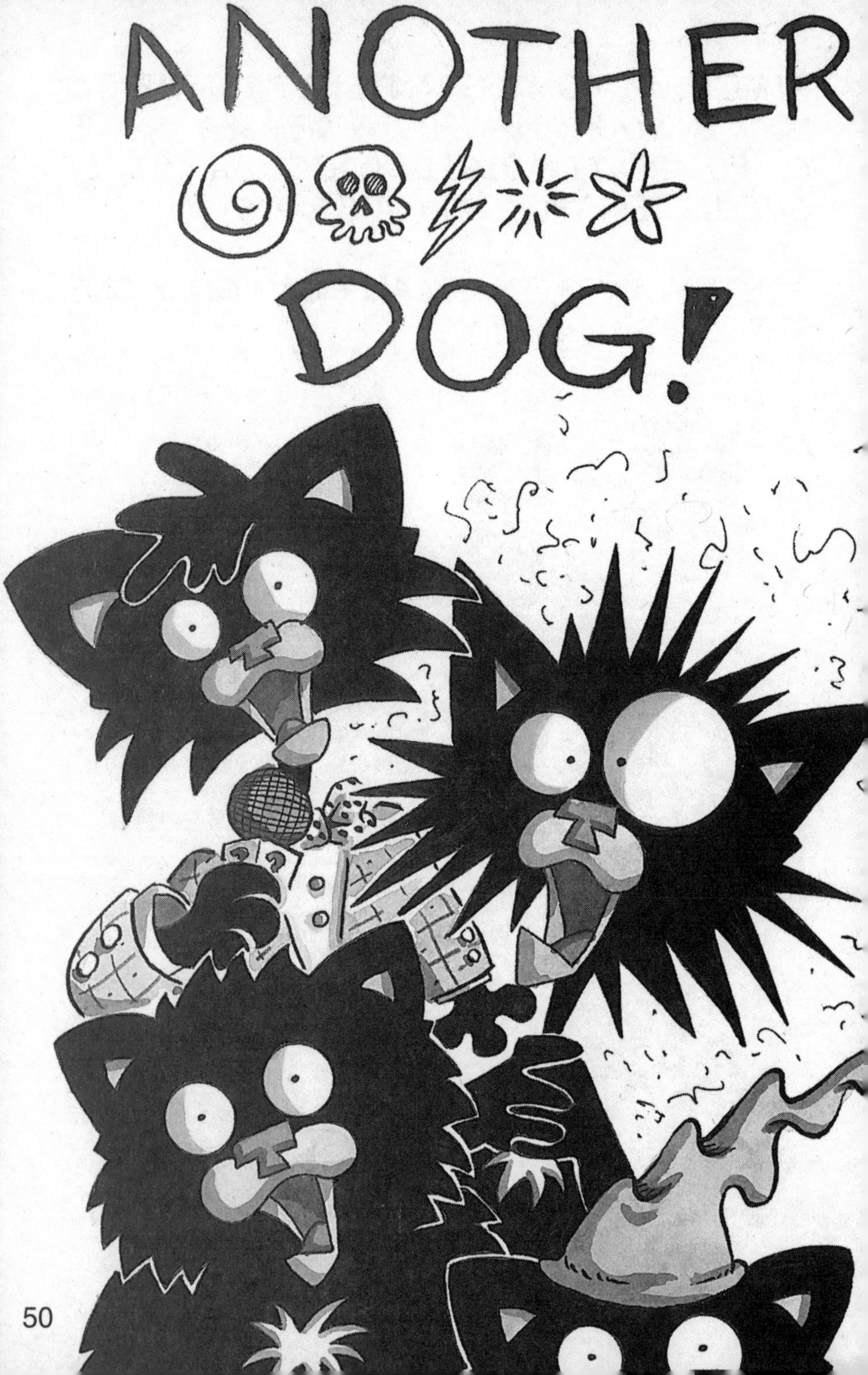
ANOTHER @☠ϟ✳✿ DOG!

•CHAPTER THREE•

ANOTHER DOG!

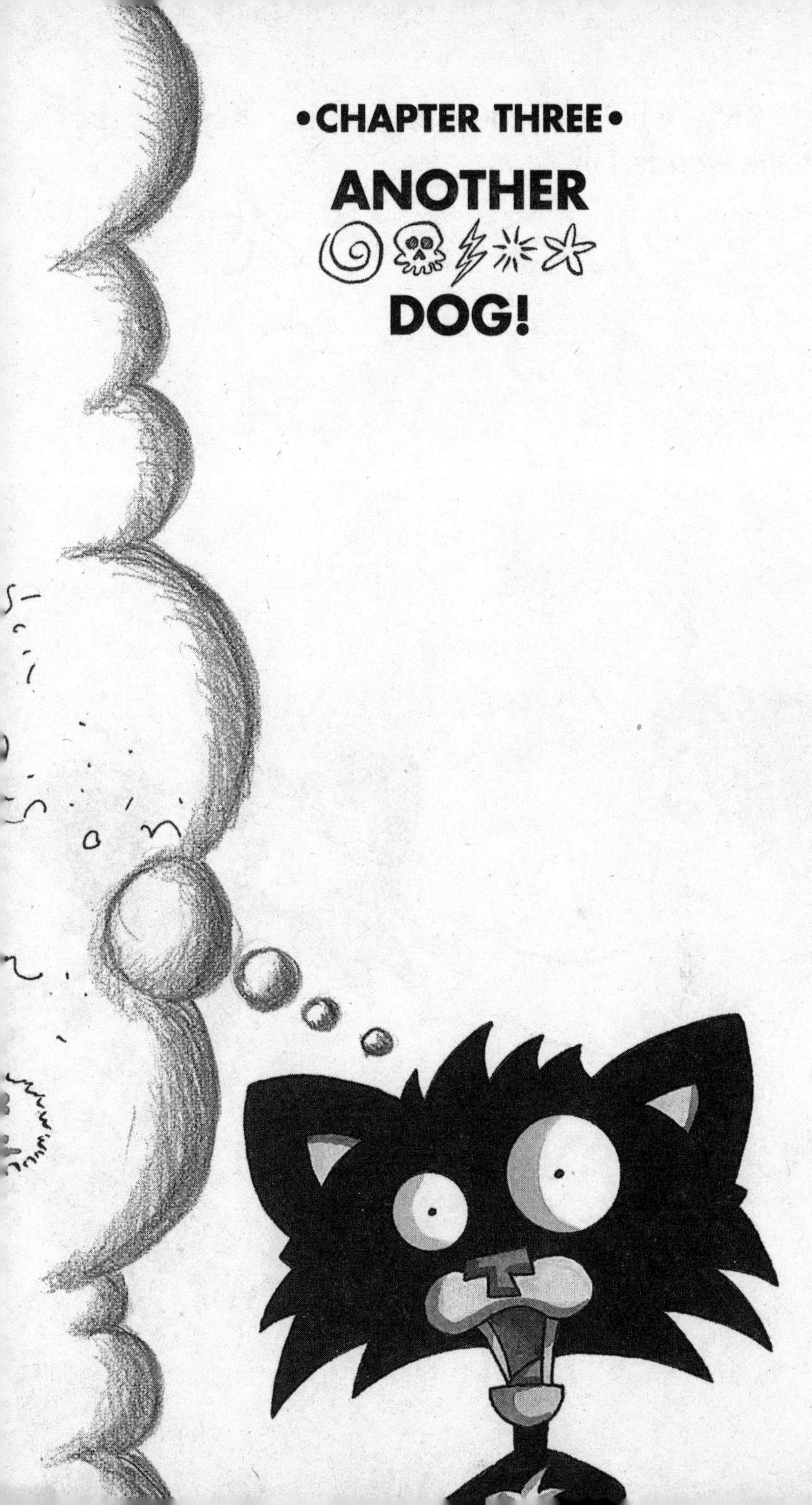

Well, Kitty, what do you think of our big surprise? Isn't she wonderful?

MEOWR REOWR
FFT FFT MEOWR
HISS FFT GROWL
REOWR HISS
HISS FFT
REOWR
GROWL FFT HISS
FFT

Oh, Kitty. Don't be like that. She's harmless. And the two of you have a lot in common. Really.

And just to prove it, I've invited all of your friends over to meet the newest addition to our family.

DING-
DONG!

Look, Kitty! It's all of the other kitties in the neighborhood! They'll prove to you that you have nothing to worry about!

*We would have been here sooner, but there was this really weird thing rolling around in the grass that could have been a snake or an armadillo or a hamburger wrapper, and we wanted to make sure that it wasn't a hamburger wrapper . . .

Awww! Isn't that sweet! They like her already. Now, aren't you ashamed of yourself, Kitty?

MEOW
MEOW
MEOW *

so we all stopped to take turns sniffing it to make sure there wasn't any hamburger left in it and there wasn't, which was upsetting at first until we realized that at least it wasn't a snake or an armadillo, whatever that is.

Look! Big Kitty is noticing how big she is!

Awww! Isn't that sweet! Big Kitty must think she's another kitty!

The Twin Kitties are noticing how much she likes to play with their cat toys. They must think she's another kitty, too.

Stinky Kitty is noticing how . . . well . . . how stinky she can be. Stinky Kitty must think she's another kitty.

Chatty Kitty is noticing how talkative she is. Chatty Kitty must think she's another kitty.

*I like chicken. I like tuna. I like mackerel. I like . . .

Pretty Kitty is noticing how soft and delicate she is.
Pretty Kitty must think she's another kitty.

What do YOU think, Strange Kitty?

In issue #189 of ASTONISHING CAT COMICS, when The Fantastic Feline Five travel across the galaxy to the Purple Panther Planet, what does the Jaguar Queen say to Mighty Manx that helps him turn his archenemy Obnoxious Ocelot into a 40-pound block of Gorgonzola cheese?

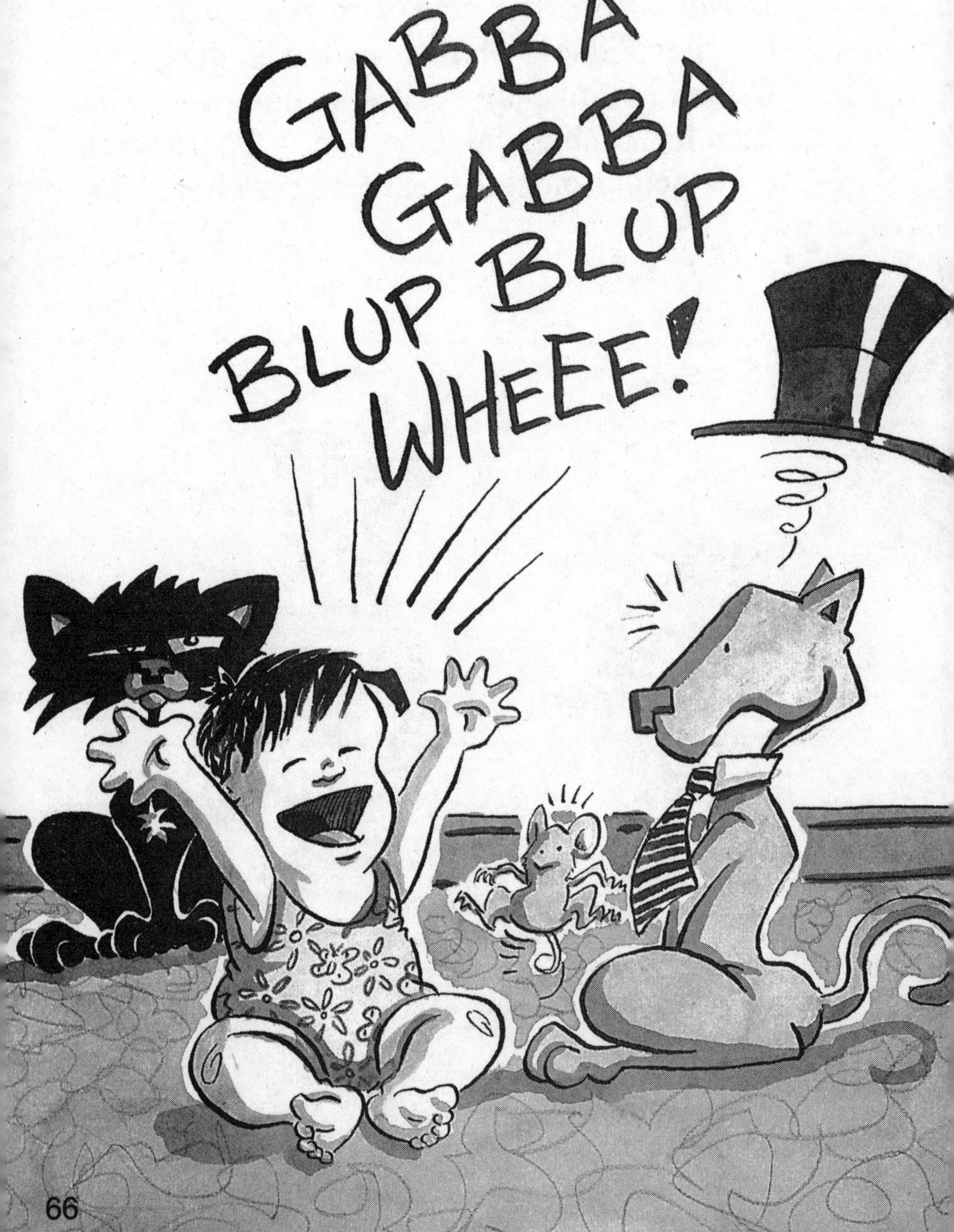
GABBA GABBA BLUP BLUP WHEEE!

Only a true kitty would have known that! So, it's official! She's one of us! And that means it's time for . . .

THE PUSSYCAT OLYMPICS!

UNCLE MURRAY'S FUN FACTS

WHY DO CATS GET STUCK IN TREES?

Do we have to do this now? I just got home, and I'm tired!

If you look at a cat's claws close up, you'll see that they all curve inward toward their paws. This means that it's very easy for a cat to climb UP something, but not so easy for it to climb back DOWN unless the cat goes backward. That might sound easy enough for you or me, but moving backward does not come naturally to cats. Think about it this way . . . When was the last time you saw a cat walk backward?

I backed that goofy cat up against a wall a few days ago, and it was one of the worst experiences of my life!

So what sometimes happens is that when a kitten or a cat who's inexperienced with climbing goes up too high, she'll realize that it's too dangerous to jump down and simply won't know what to do. What's worse is that a frightened cat will often keep climbing higher and higher in the tree to find a different way down.

Which is not at all like what happened to me when I got stuck in the tree. See, I kept climbing up and up thinking that the higher you get in the tree, the longer the branches get. And eventually I'd find a branch long enough to get me back down. Makes sense, right?

69

CHAPTER FOUR

THE PUSSYCAT OLYMPICS

Well, old chum, it's a beautiful day here inside the living room and I can think of no better way to celebrate the arrival of this new kitty than by once again holding . . .

THE PUSSYCAT OLYMPICS!

Conditions simply could not be better for these games, S.K. This carpet was vacuumed just two days ago!

The athletes are entering the room!
And what a colorful group they are!

I know I say this every time,
S.K., but this is always my
favorite part of these games.

Here comes Big Kitty! You can
tell that he's been training.

The Twin Kitties look eager to compete.
True champions, the both of them.

Pretty Kitty is looking as lovely as ever! *sigh*

And just behind her, Stinky Kitty is looking as filthy as ever! *Ack!*

Here comes Chatty Kitty, trying to psyche out the competition as usual.

And here comes our host kitty! Wow! I don't know if I've ever seen such a look of determination on an athlete's face. This could mean trouble!

MEOW MEOW *

*Did you know that the first parade was really just a bunch of rocks that were all rolling down a hill at the same time and fell into a tuba? It's true! I looked it up.

 And following her is the New Kitty. What do you think we can expect from this newcomer?

 Hard to say, S.K. She's a plucky, young go-getter with a will to win. That much is for sure.

This could get exciting, folks! LET THE GAMES BEGIN!

This first event is always a crowd pleaser! It's the STARE-AT-YOUR-SELF-IN-A-MIRROR-UNTIL-YOU-GET-BORED competition. Pretty Kitty remains undefeated in this event, but Stinky Kitty has promised to give her a challenge.

Pretty Kitty's looking good, S.K. And I mean very, VERY good. *sigh* Couldn't you just swim in those big, dark, beautiful eyes? And her fur— so soft . . . so velvety . . .

Sorry to interrupt, but something is happening out on the floor!

 Stinky Kitty is asleep! I think he's always been asleep! That means he's automatically disqualified! And that means this contest is just between . . .

Hold that thought, S.K.! Something else is happening!

 WOW! Pretty Kitty was momentarily distracted! And that means that in a stunning upset, the NEW KITTY IS THE WINNER!

S.K., I'm here in the living room talking with the winner.

That was an incredible display, New Kitty. Can you give us some insight into your training program?

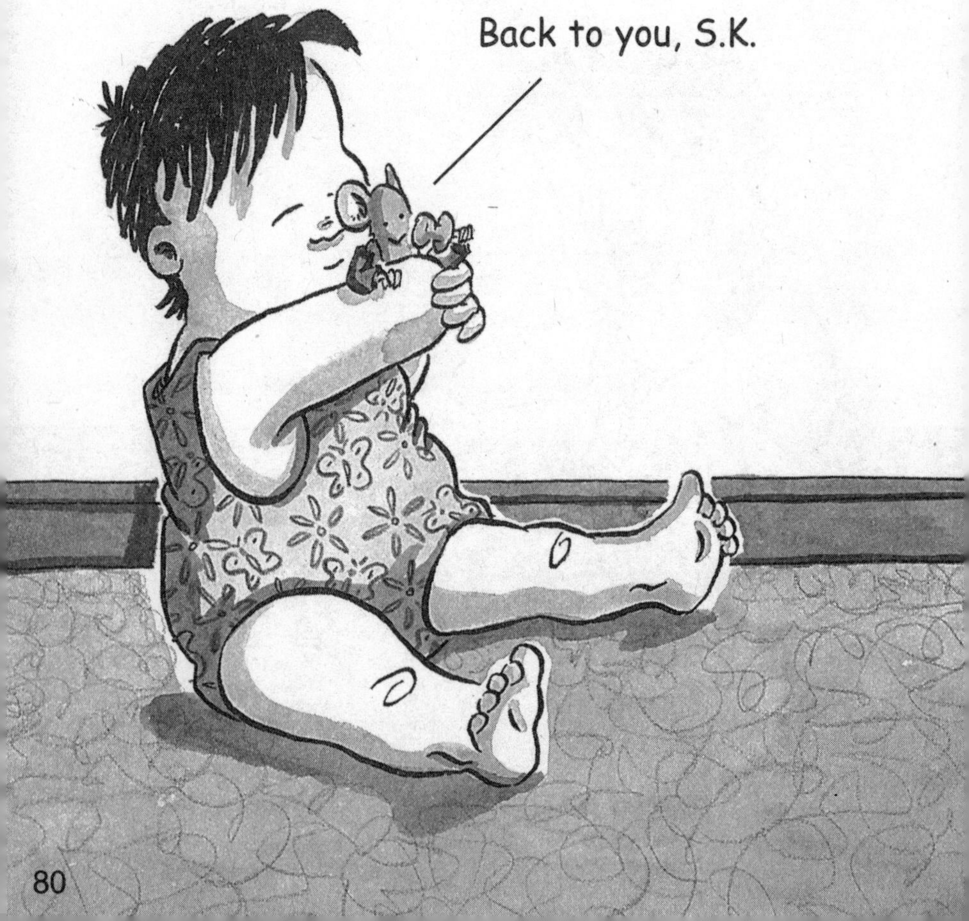
Back to you, S.K.

The BABBLING-ON-AND-ON-WITHOUT-STOPPING event has been Chatty Kitty's domain for many years now. But Big Kitty is hoping for an upset today. And apparently so is our ambitious young newcomer, fresh from her recent victory. Let's watch the action!

MEOW
MEOW

MEOW
MEOW
MEOW
MEOW
MEOW*

BA
BA
BA
BA
BA

*I was watching television last week when someone—I think he was either an actor or a doctor or an actor who plays a doctor on a TV show or a doctor who plays an actor on a TV show, but that doesn't make any sense—said that eggs were good for a cat's fur, which sounded just gross because I think your fur would get all sticky and weird if you rubbed eggs on yourself.

This could go on for hours, folks. So feel free to step into another room to get a drink of water or find some cotton for your ears or . . .

MEOW

MEOW
MEOW
MEOW
MEOW*

BA
BA
BA
BA
BA

*He might have meant that you had to cook the eggs first, but how would you cook them? It might feel nice if you scrambled them, but that could still get messy, and hard-boiled eggs would feel kind of odd even if you peeled them. I think fried eggs would be the kind of eggs I would put on my fur because they would probably stick there the longest until, of course, it rained and then I would . . .

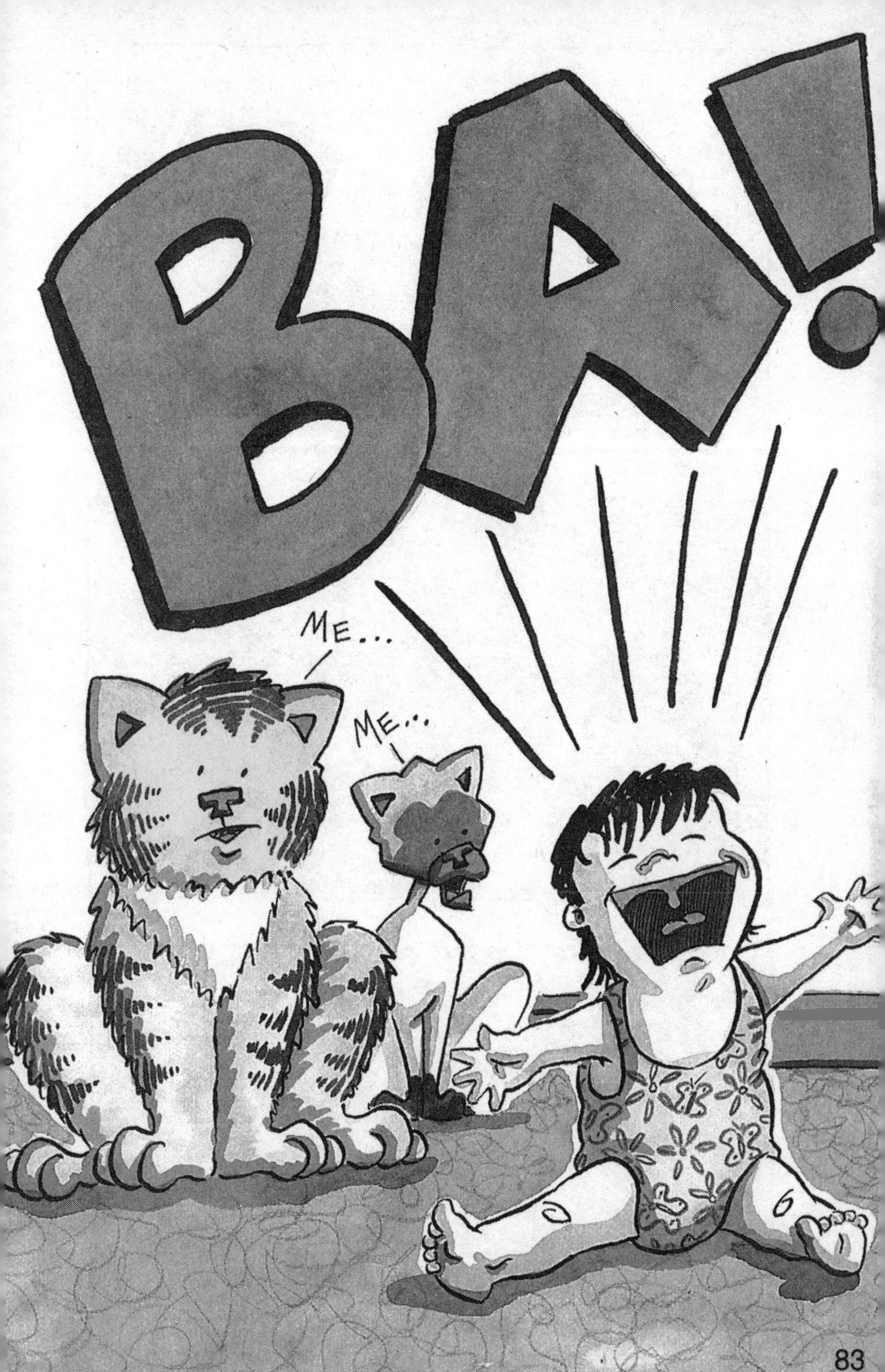
BA!
ME...
ME...

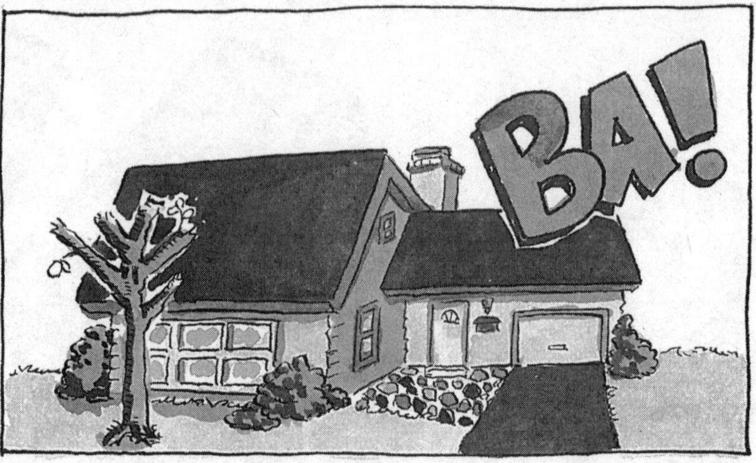
BA!

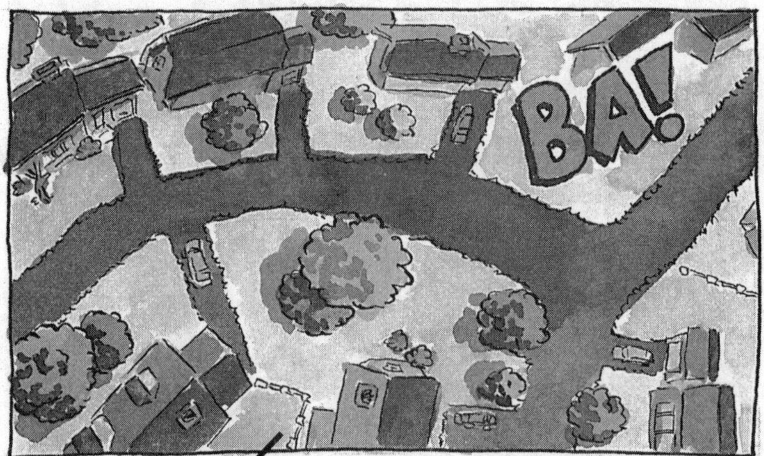
BA!

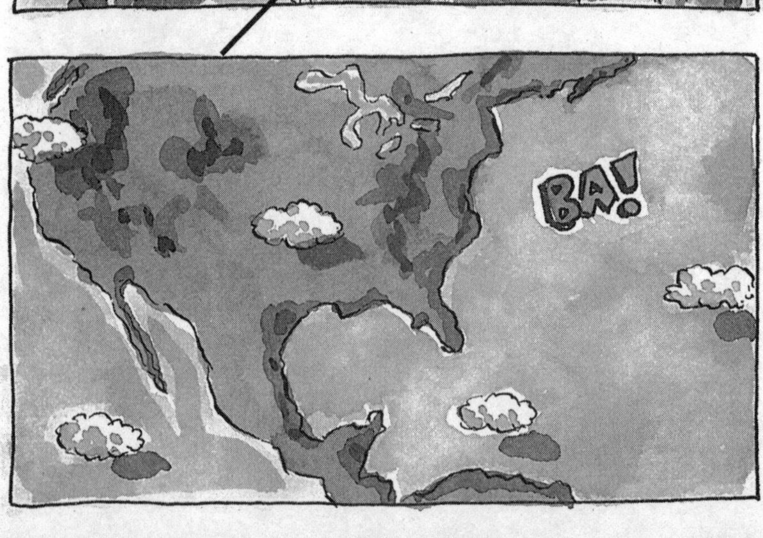
BA!

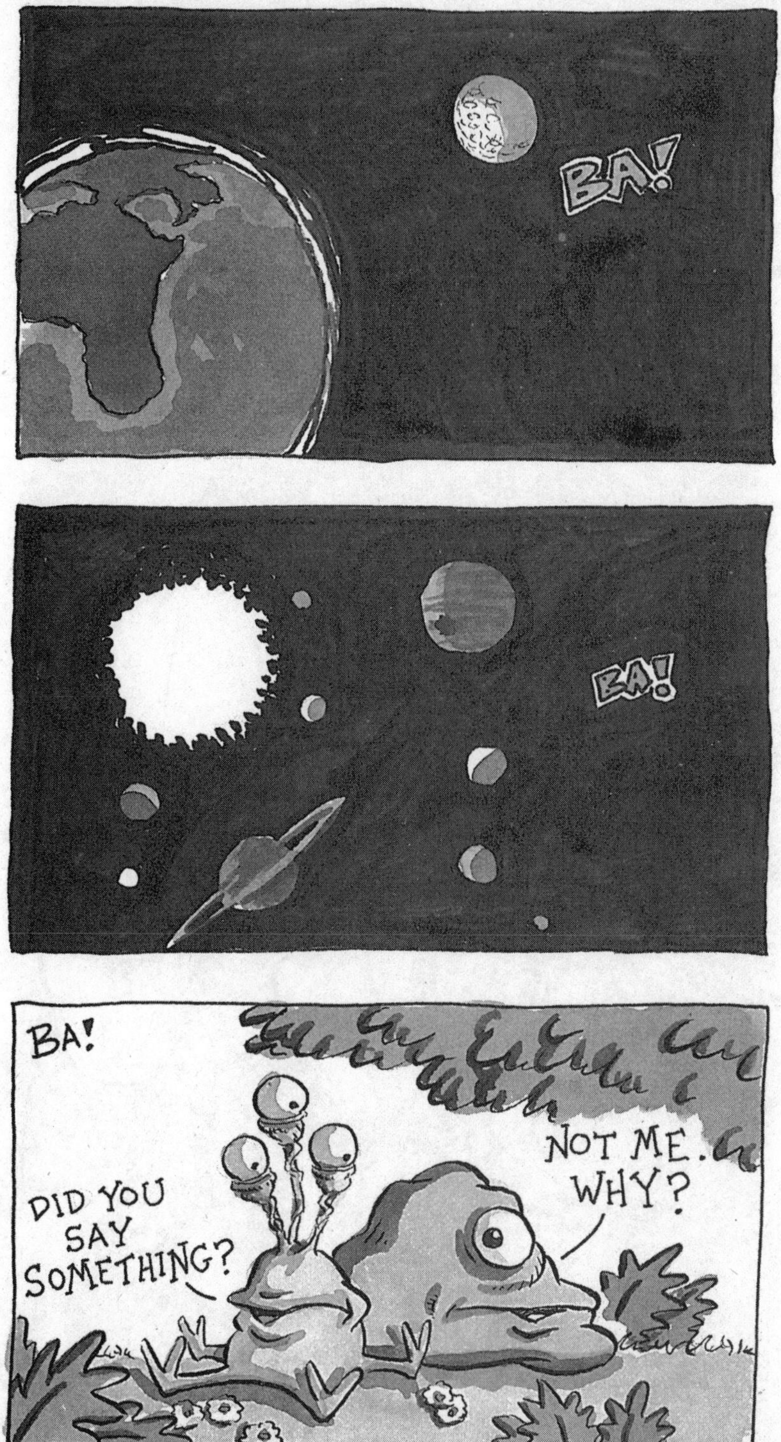
BA!
BA!
BA!
DID YOU SAY SOMETHING?
NOT ME. WHY?

 Big Kitty and Chatty Kitty have both been left speechless! Speechless! What a stunning victory for New Kitty!

Well, folks, despite protests from the neighbors, it's time once again for the WHO-CAN-CREATE-THE-BIGGEST-STINK event, also known as the WHO-CAN-OUTSTINK-STINKY-KITTY competition. This is a grueling event that's not for the faint of heart.

The Twin Kitties took up the challenge this year. Rumor has it that they rolled around in the dumpster behind a seafood restaurant and bathed in garlic juice just before the event.

But, as expected, even the Twin Kitties look overcome by the inspiringly putrid essence of Stinky Kitty. This event is just about over.

 But wait! New Kitty is entering the playing field! Could this amazing athlete really pose a challenge to Stinky Kitty?

What could she possibly do this late in the game? What could she possibly do that could emit such a noxious odor big enough to . . .

NNNNNNG...

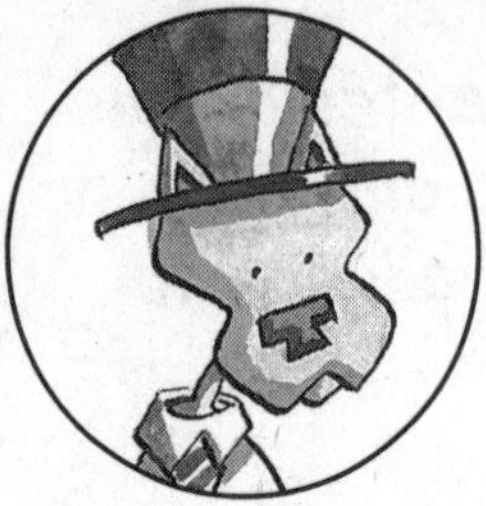

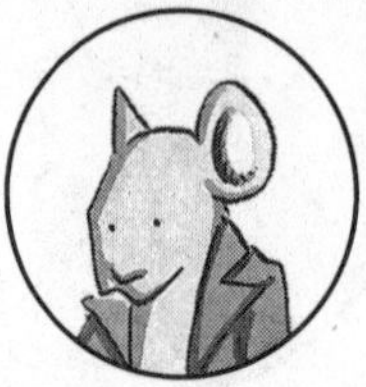

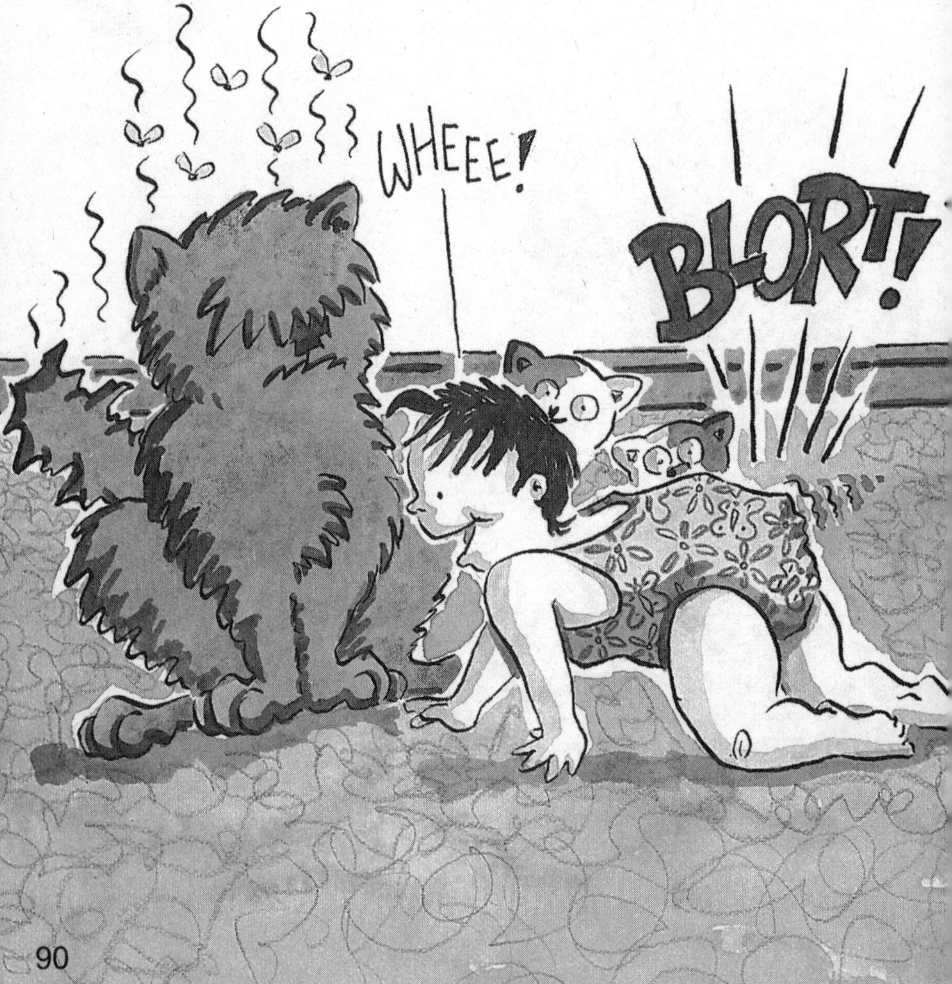
WHEEE!
BLORT!

What an amazing athlete! What an amazing kitty! What a true champion! What a stunning defeat for Stinky Kitty! A new era has come! This day will go down in history!

S.K., I'm down here once again with the winner—the winner of not just one but ALL THREE of the events played today . . . except that . . . I'm starting to feel a little lightheaded . . . and I think I should sit down . . . seeing spots . . . everything's going black . . .

WHEW! I think it's time to change your diaper, young lady. And then we'll get you something to eat.

93

And now it's time for the last event of the day, the one we've all been waiting for. Some would call this the most challenging of all the events in The Pussycat Olympics. Surely, it is the one event that separates the cats from the kittens. I'm speaking, of course, of THE EATING CONTEST!

And no other kitty in the history of The Pussycat Olympics has ever dominated this sport more than our host. Time and time again, she has consumed more food than could ever be imagined. Time and time again, she has proved that no meal is too large, no food bowl too deep, no menu too absurd for this kitty and her extraordinary appetite.

SUPPER TIME, KITTY!

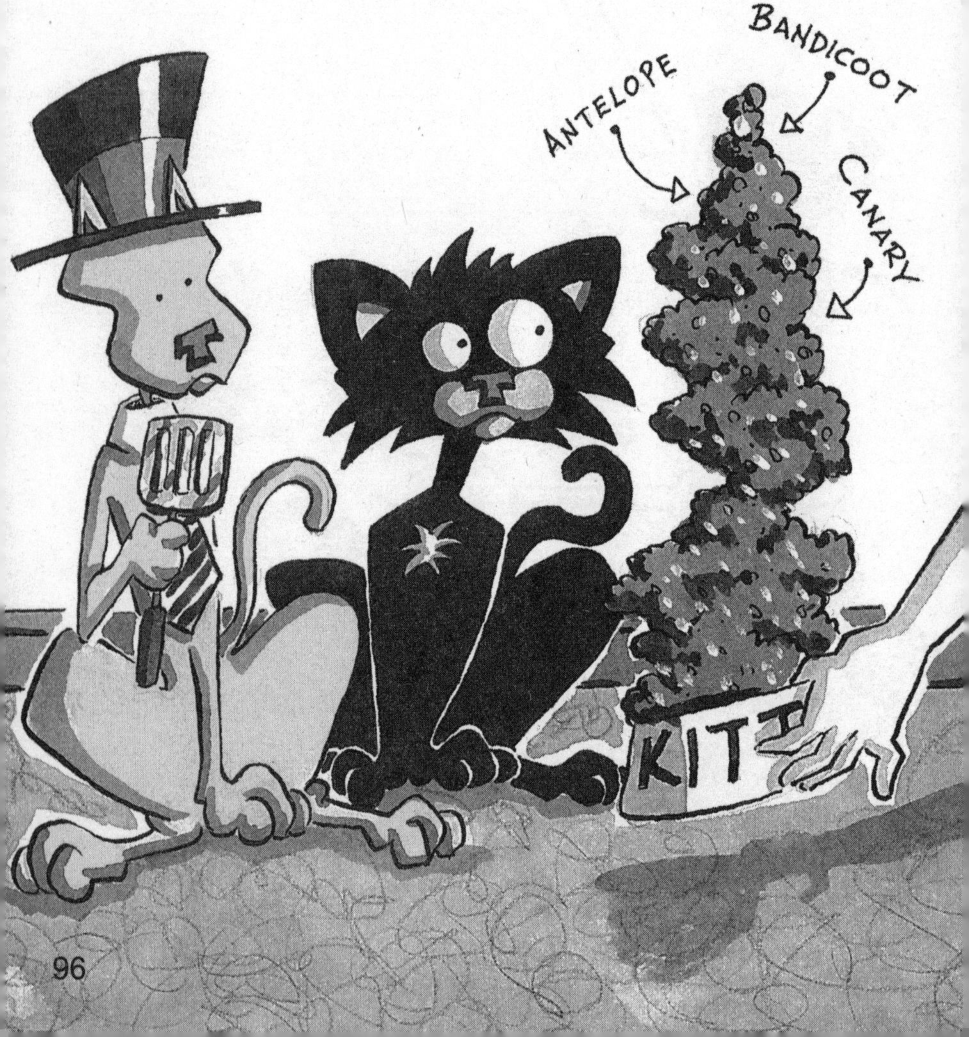

ANTELOPE
BANDICOOT
CANARY
KITT

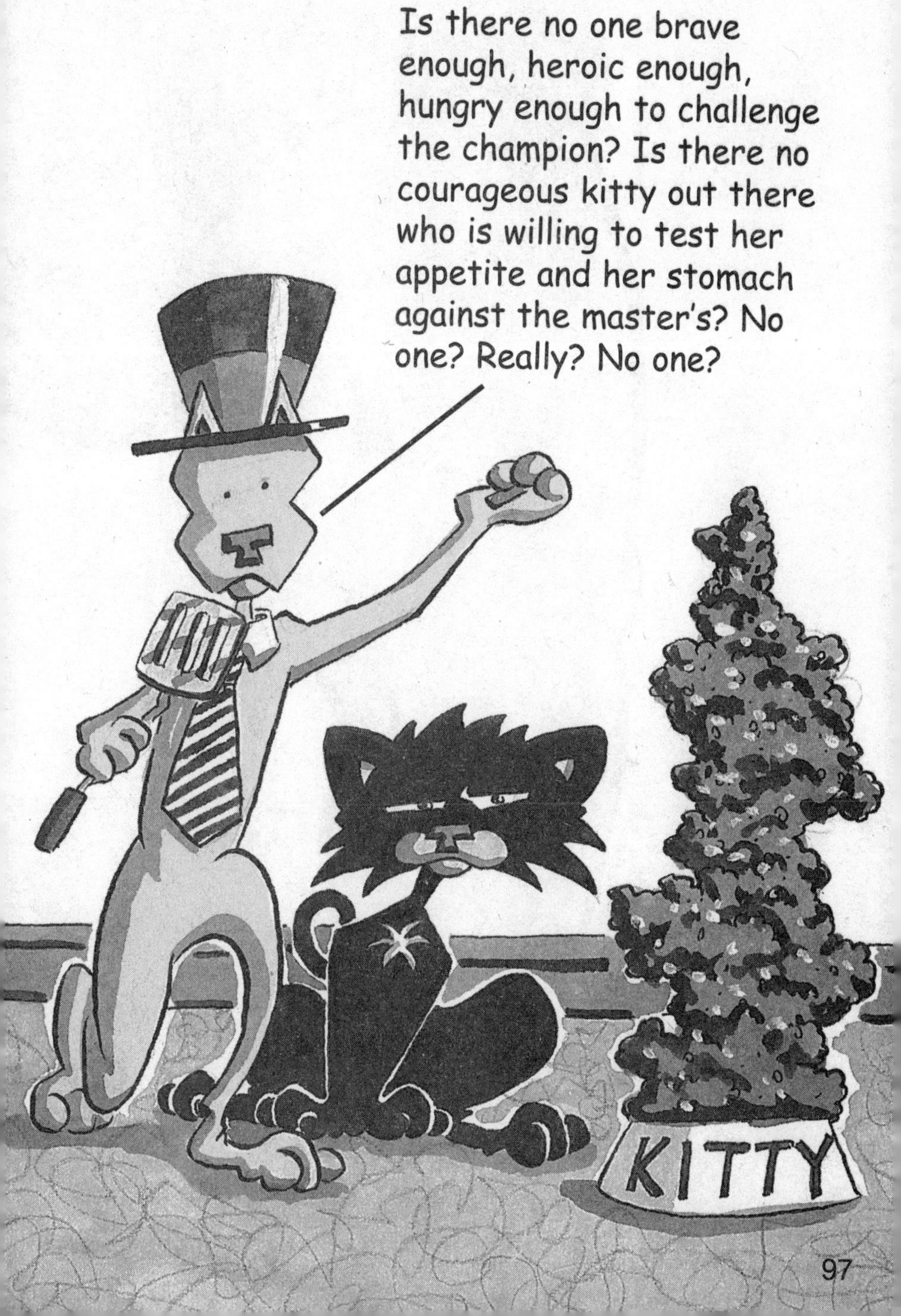
Is there no one brave enough, heroic enough, hungry enough to challenge the champion? Is there no courageous kitty out there who is willing to test her appetite and her stomach against the master's? No one? Really? No one?
KITTY

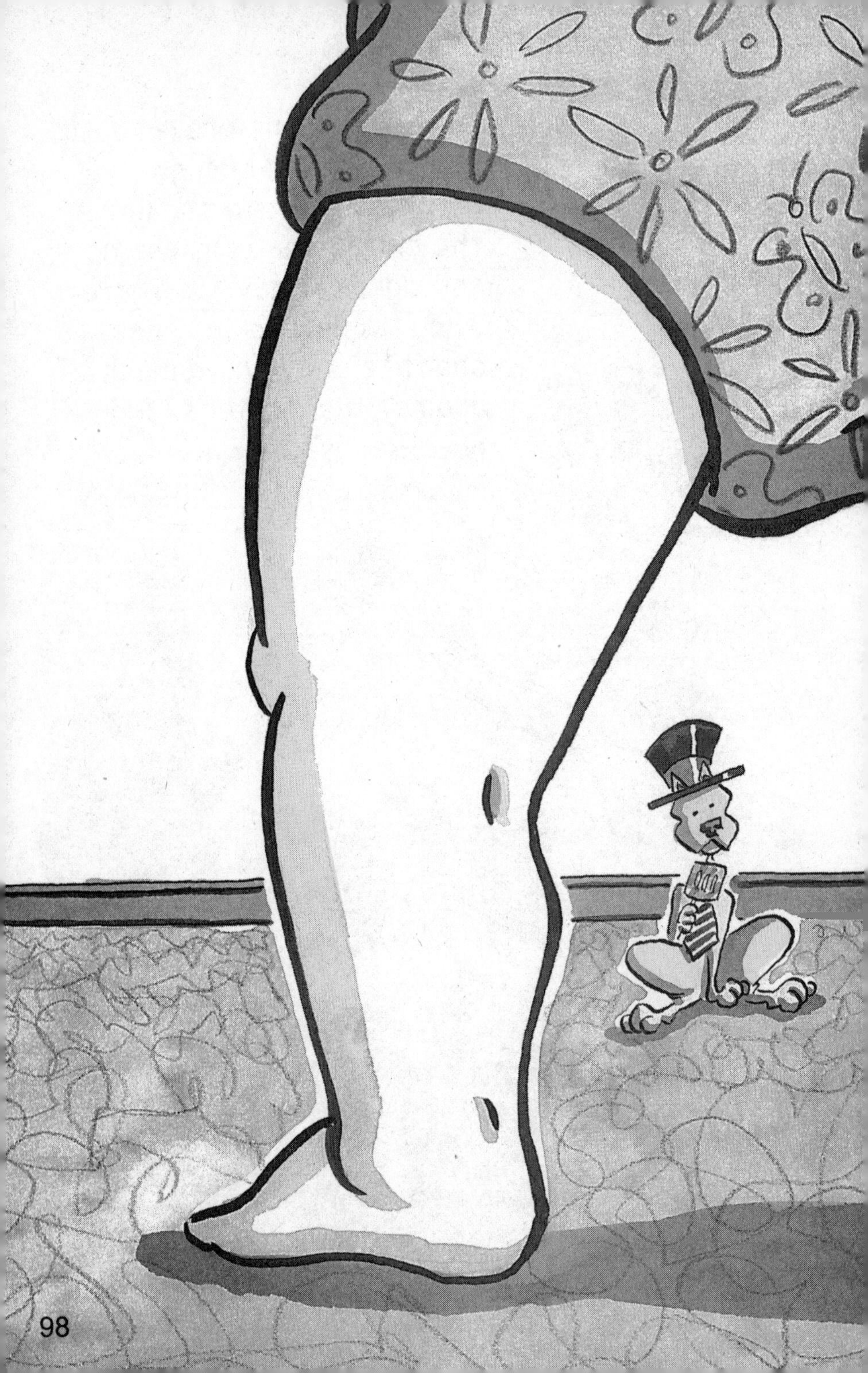

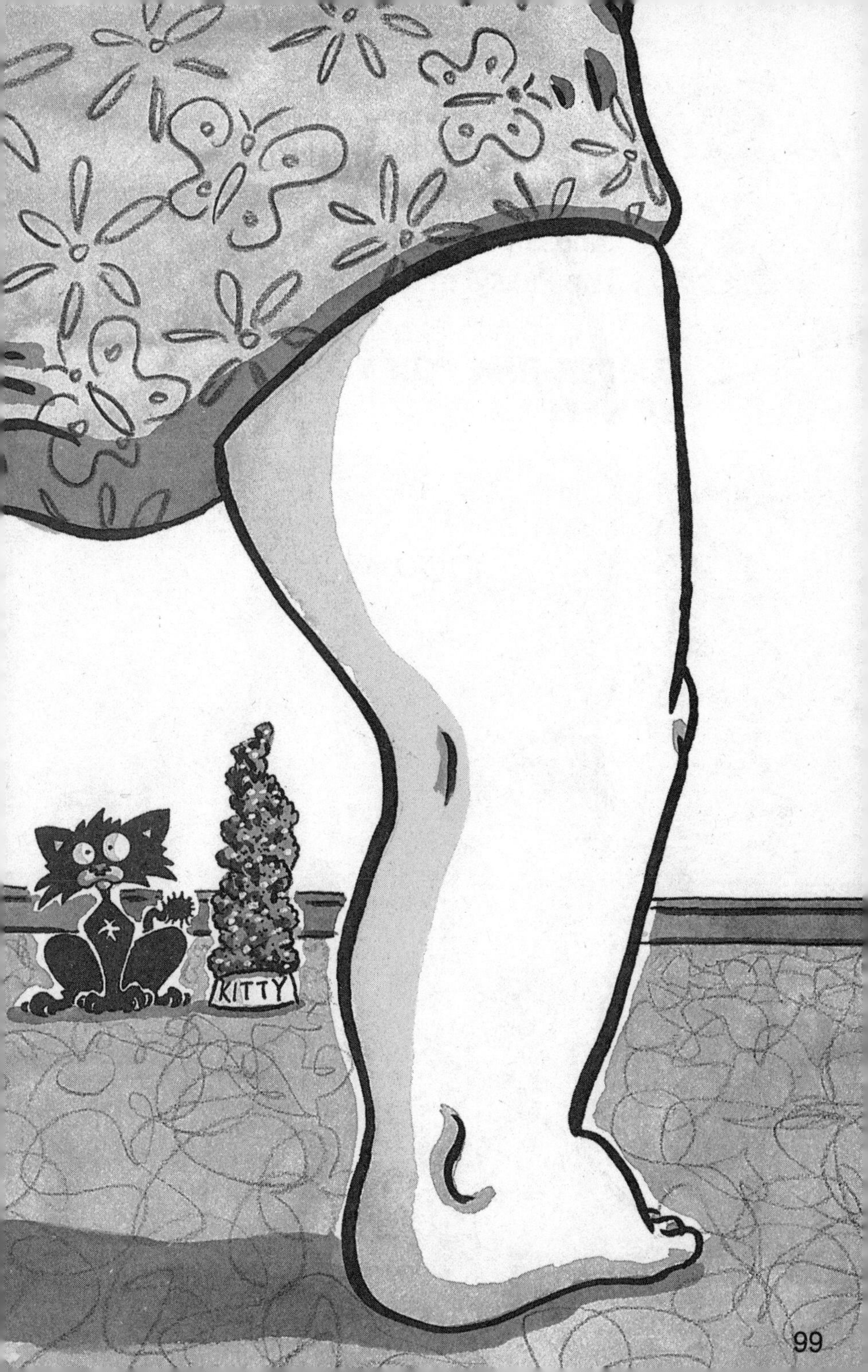
KITTY

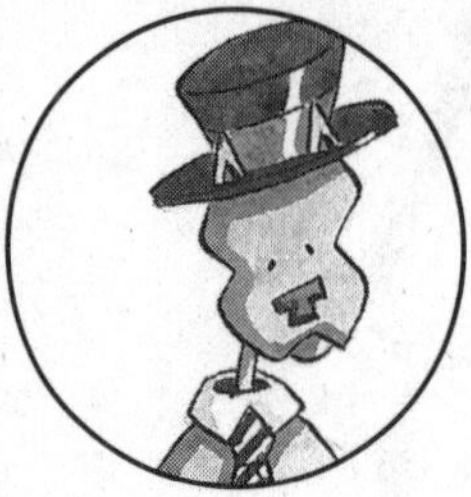

Could it be . . . ? Is it . . . ? YES, IT IS! It's none other than the New Kitty! Could she perform the impossible and win EVERY event in The Pussycat Olympics?

SUPPER TIME FOR YOU, TOO, HONEY!

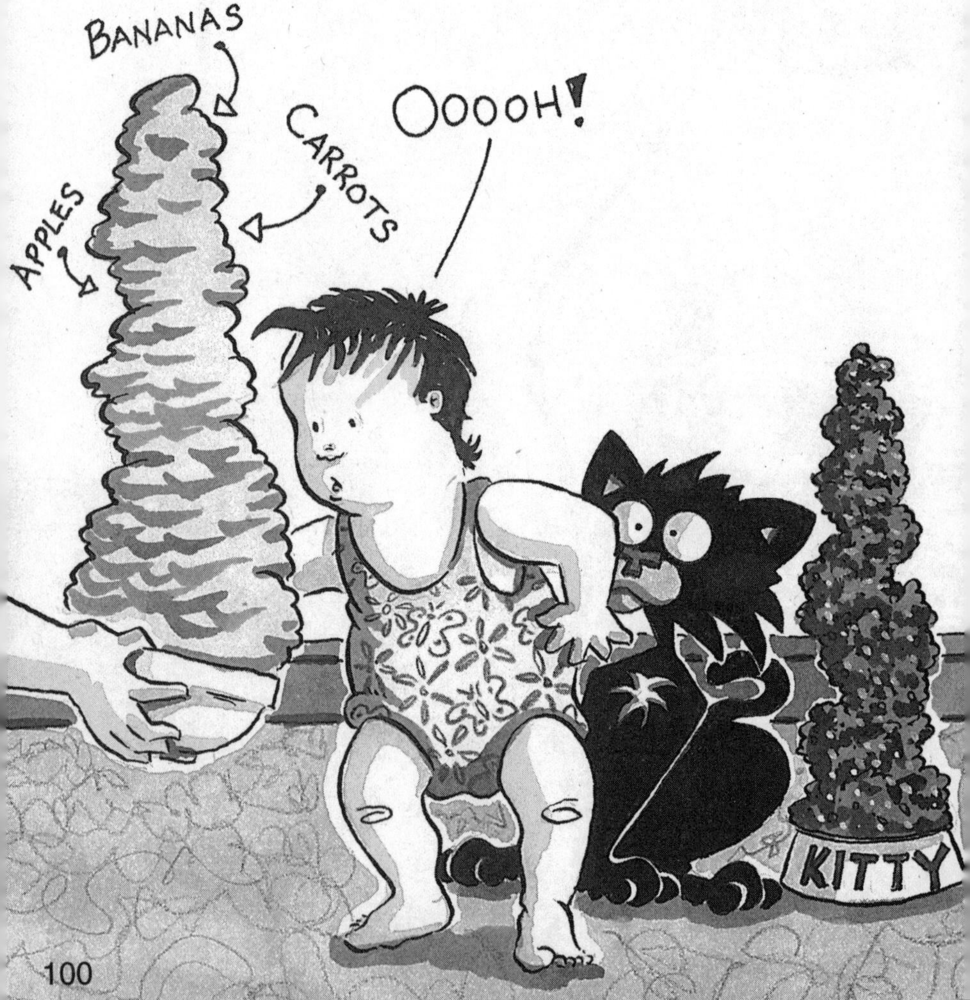
BANANAS
CARROTS
APPLES
OOOOH!
KITTY

Okay, athletes! You know the rules! Whoever finishes her bowl of food first wins!

ON YOUR MARK . . .

GET SET . . .

GO!

101

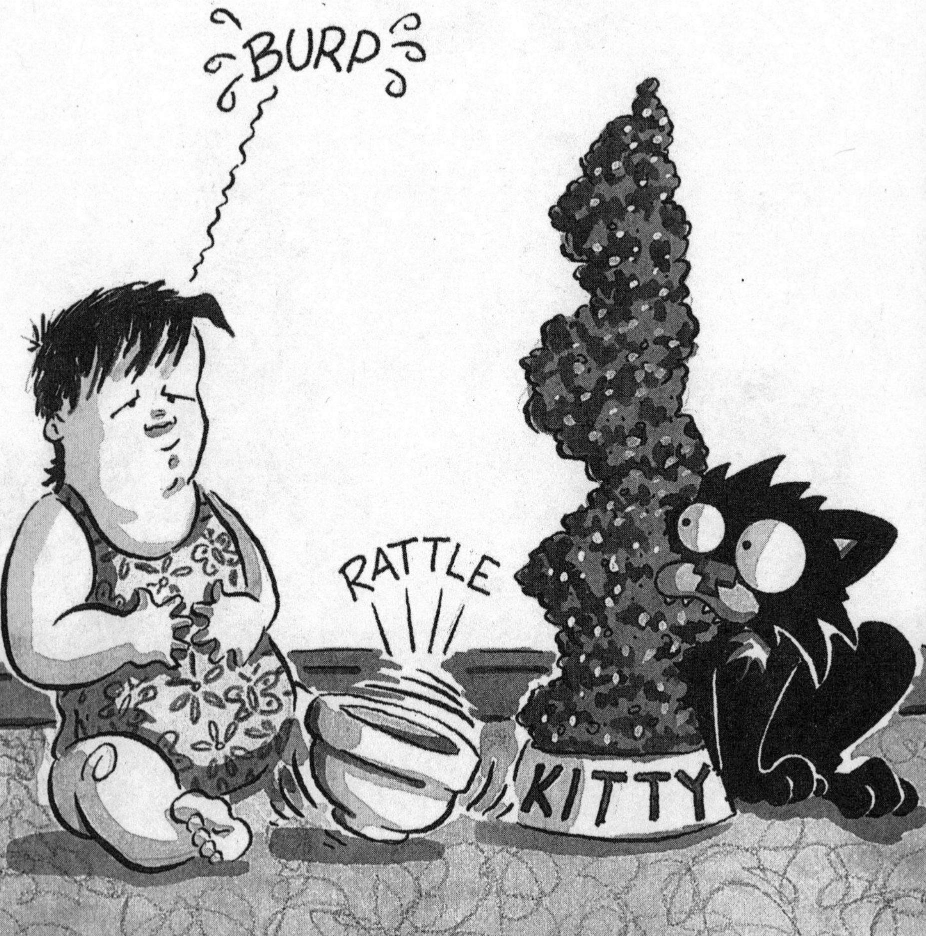
BURP
RATTLE
KITTY

WHAT AN INCREDIBLE PERFORMANCE! NEW KITTY HAS DONE THE IMPOSSIBLE AND WON EVERY SINGLE EVENT IN THE PUSSYCAT OLYMPICS!

She's more than just a kitty, she's a SUPER KITTY!

S.K., I'm feeling much better and am here speaking with the winner.

That was an extraordinary performance today, New Kitty. To what do you owe your amazing abilities?

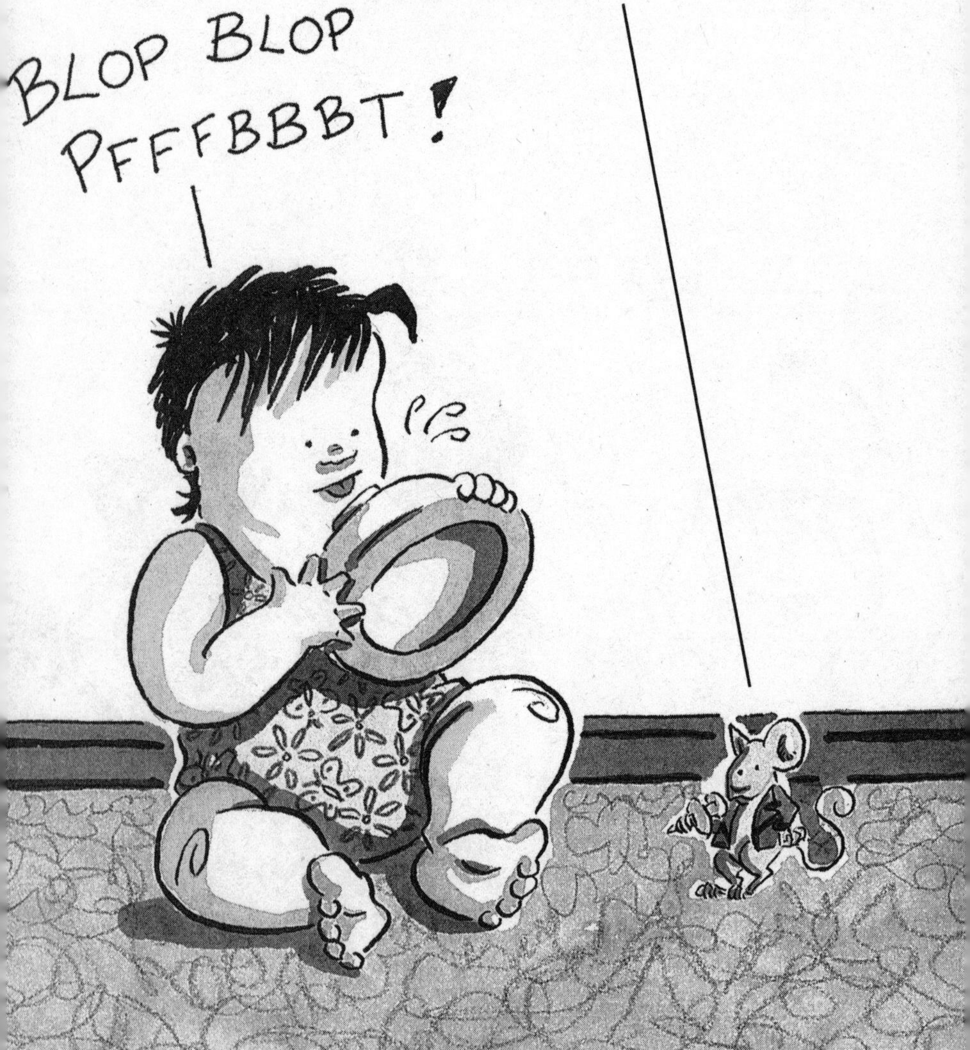
BLOP BLOP
PFFFBBBT!

Truer words
have never
been spoken.

Ouch.

105

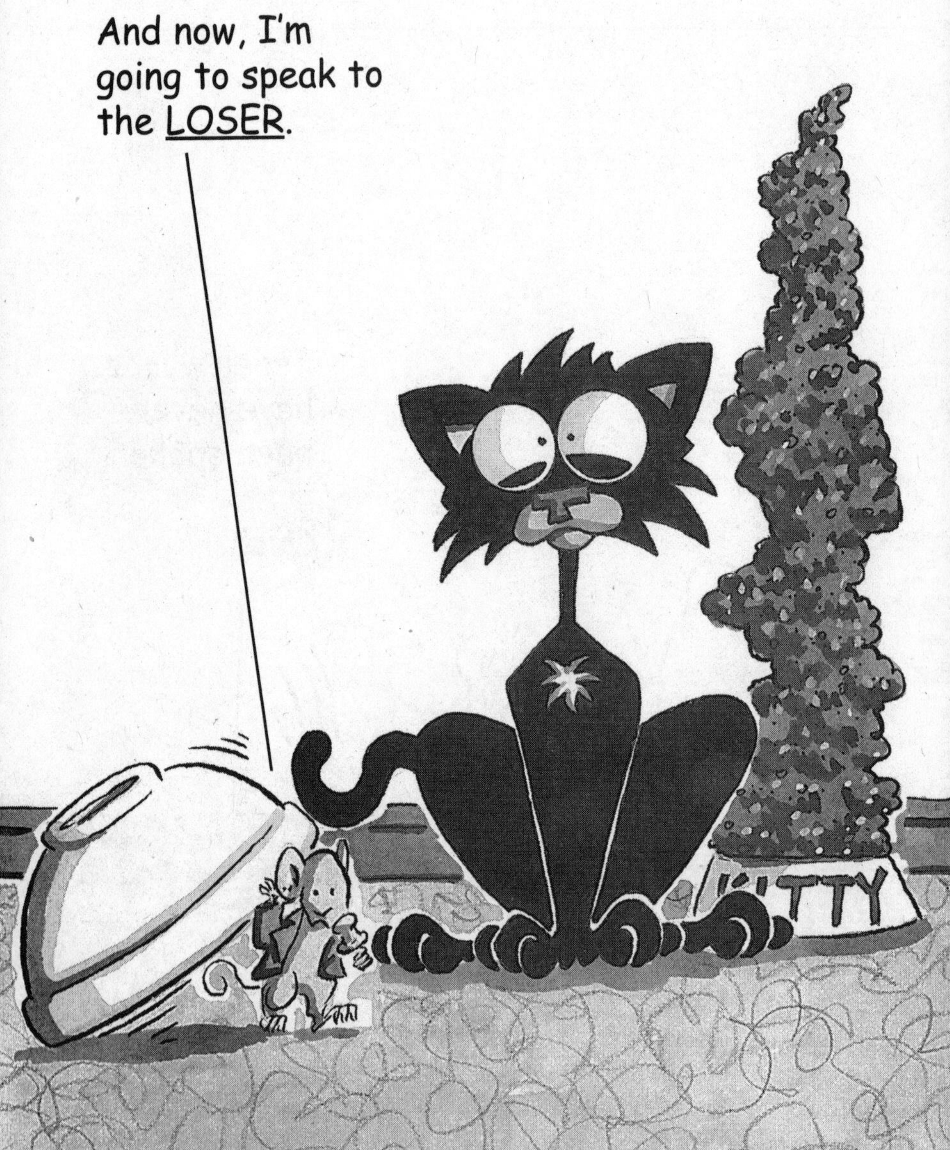
And now, I'm going to speak to the LOSER.
KITTY

Tell us . . . now that you've <u>LOST</u>, can you tell our audience how it feels to have <u>LOST</u> because this is the first time you've ever <u>LOST</u> this event. Plus, you <u>LOST</u> to a newcomer.

I mean . . . you didn't just <u>LOSE</u>, you know, you <u>LOST</u> by a lot! You didn't even come close! I saw the whole thing, and it was a pretty incredible <u>LOSS</u>. Were you even trying? Because you <u>LOST</u> pretty big time there!

Which is to say . . . um . . . that . . . do
you have any . . . uh . . . comments . . . ?
Anything . . . ? Anything at all . . . ?
Nothing . . . ? Really?

Uh-oh.

*Look out! Gangway! Move it or lose it!

Thank you for joining us for The Pussycat Olympics. We now bring you our regularly scheduled screaming temper tantrum.

CHAPTER FIVE

OUR REGULARLY SCHEDULED SCREAMING TEMPER TANTRUM

Well, Kitty . . . You've done it again. Everyone was having such a nice time until you had to go and spoil it by freaking out. And why? Because you lost a few little games.

We love you, Kitty, but sometimes you're not just a **Bad Kitty**. Sometimes you're a bad loser, too.

No, Kitty. It's not her fault. It's nobody's fault but your own.

Now where do you think you're going?

No, Kitty. She's not moving out. She's staying here with us whether you like it or not.

Sigh No, Kitty. We can't ship her back to where she came from.

No, Kitty. We're not going to sell her either. Now stop it!

Kitty, I just don't understand why you're acting so badly. The two of you have so much in common. You both like to scratch things. You both like to chew on things you shouldn't. You obviously both like to eat a lot.

And you're both adopted.

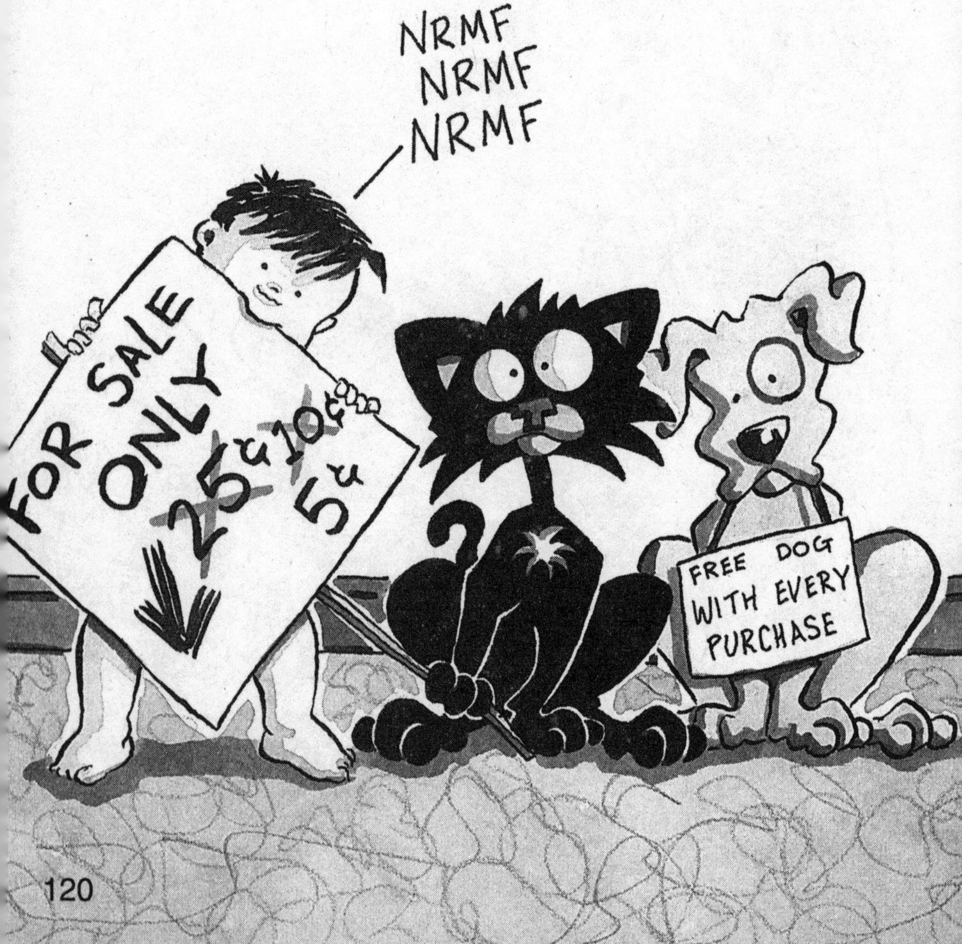
NRMF
NRMF
NRMF
FOR SALE
ONLY
25¢ 10¢
5¢
FREE DOG
WITH EVERY
PURCHASE

That's right, Kitty. This baby needed someone to feed her. This baby needed someone to read her stories and play with her. This baby needed someone to love her and take good care of her—just like you and Puppy once needed all of those things.

And this baby needed a place to live that was warm and safe and happy just like you and Puppy once needed this place.

This baby needed a home just like you and Puppy once needed a home. And now she has all that . . .

FREE DOG WITH EVERY PURCHASE

Just like you.

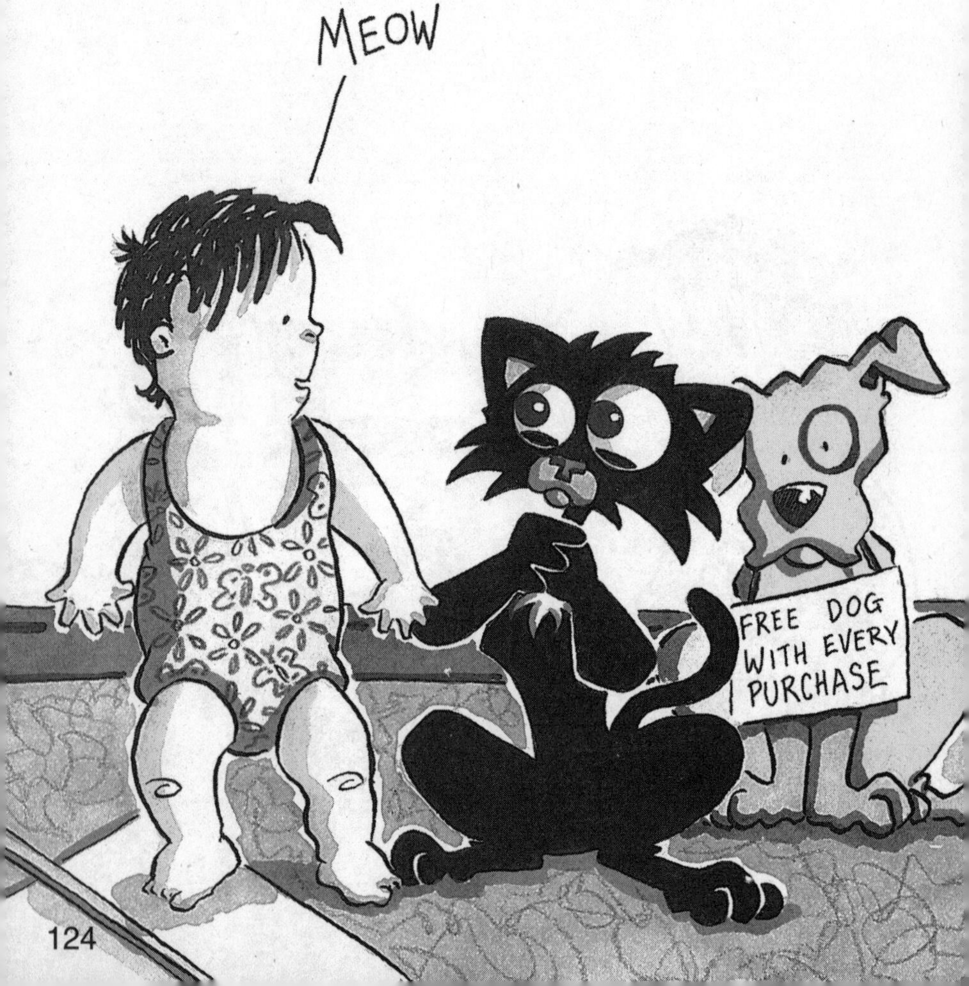
MEOW
FREE DOG WITH EVERY PURCHASE

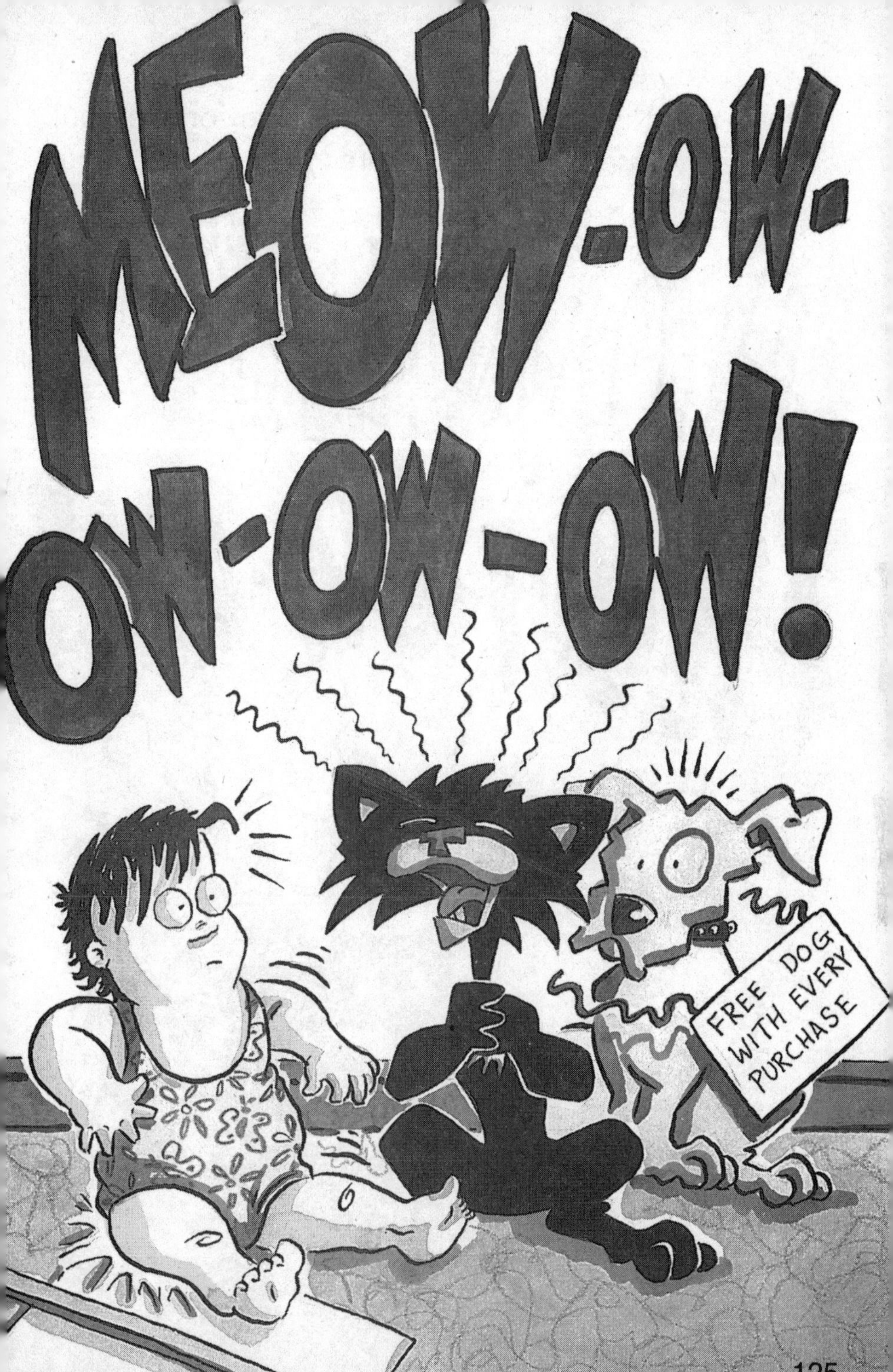
MEOW-OW-OW-
OW-OW-OW-OW!
FREE DOG WITH EVERY PURCHASE

Listen, you two, if you don't stop all this caterwauling and howling right now, you're going to make the baby . . .

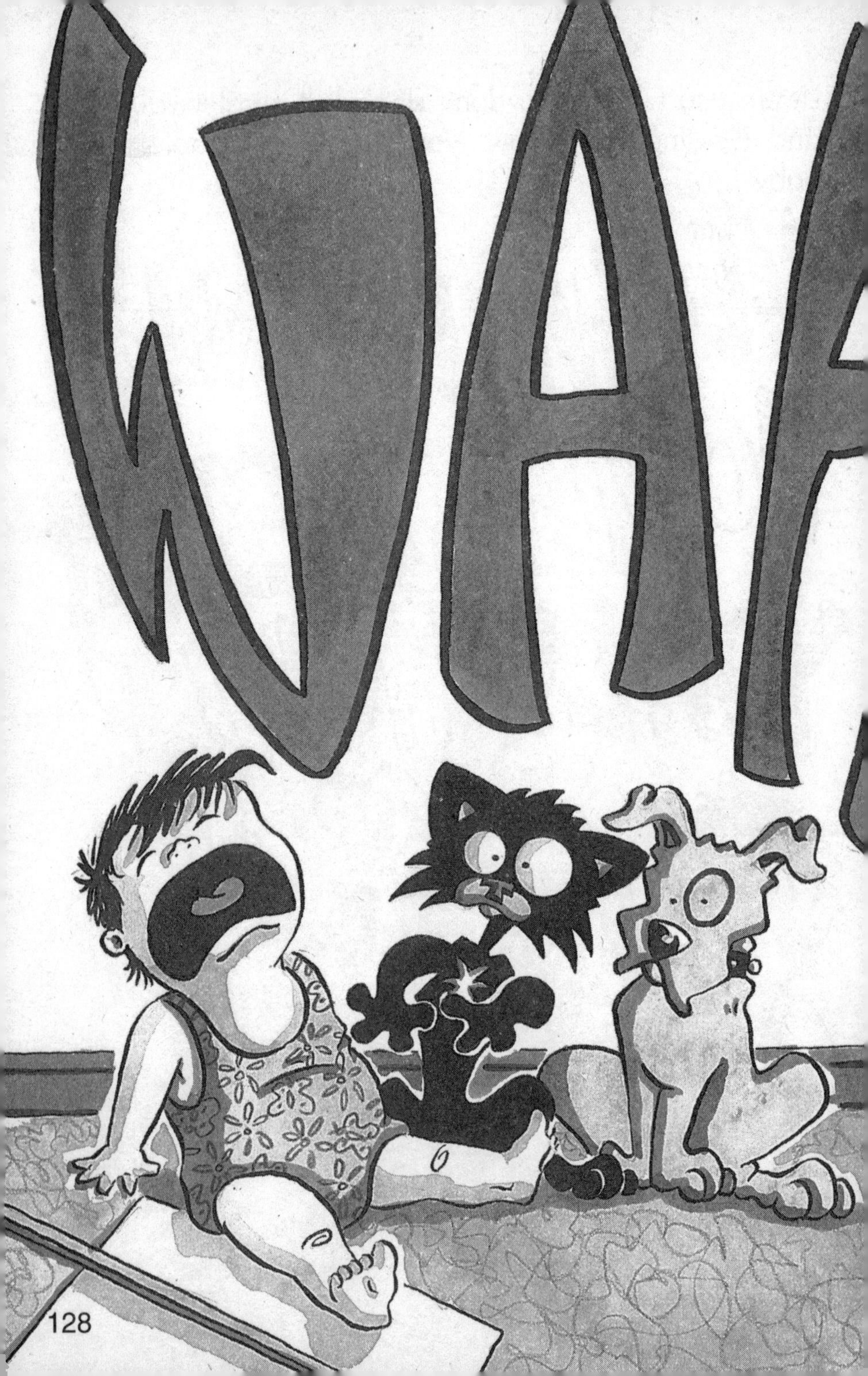
WA

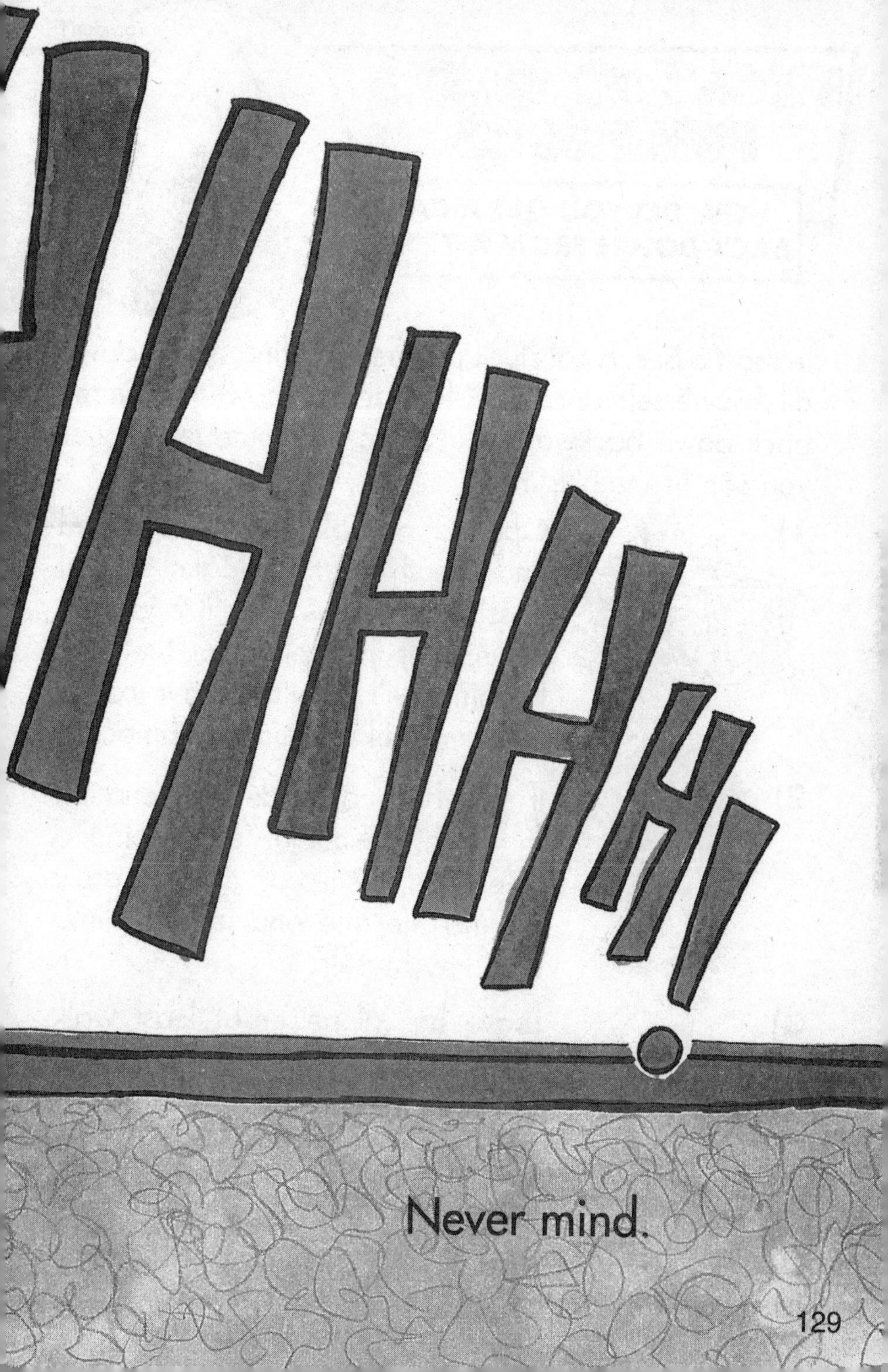
HHHHH!

Never mind.

You don't! Life's too short!

UNCLE MURRAY'S FUN FACTS

HOW DO YOU GET A CAT BACK DOWN FROM A TREE?

In most cases, a cat stuck in a tree will find a way down all by herself once she figures out how to shimmy back down backward. But there are some techniques you can use to help her.

1)  Open a can of her favorite food underneath the tree. Make sure, if possible, that she sees it and then leave it at the bottom of the tree. Nothing will convince your cat to take a risk like a hungry stomach.

2)  If you have a ladder tall enough to reach the cat or even come a little close, then prop it up securely against the tree and let her climb down by herself.

3)  Leave her alone or at least walk away from the tree. Sometimes even your best intentions might make your cat even more nervous during this awful experience. Letting her find the food or the ladder by herself could be the best tactic.

But if hours pass or it's starting to get dark or cold outside, then it might be time to take matters into your own hands. If the cat isn't too high up and if your ladder is sturdy enough, put on a thick coat and a pair of thick work gloves and go on up to get her. Move slowly so you don't make her more nervous. Try to grab her by the scruff of the neck. Even though cats hate this, you'll need your other hand to climb back down.

If the situation becomes a real emergency or if the cat is just too high up to reach by yourself, avoid calling the fire department if at all possible. Despite their reputation, many fire departments have a strict policy against cat rescues. This is because the time spent rescuing a cat from a tree could distract them from a fire that could be taking place elsewhere.

Instead, call your local animal shelter or humane society. They're the real professionals for this sort of thing.

Great. Now you tell me.

•CHAPTER SIX•
A NEW BEGINNING

Well, Kitty. I guess it's nice that you've become so close to the baby.

But sometimes . . .

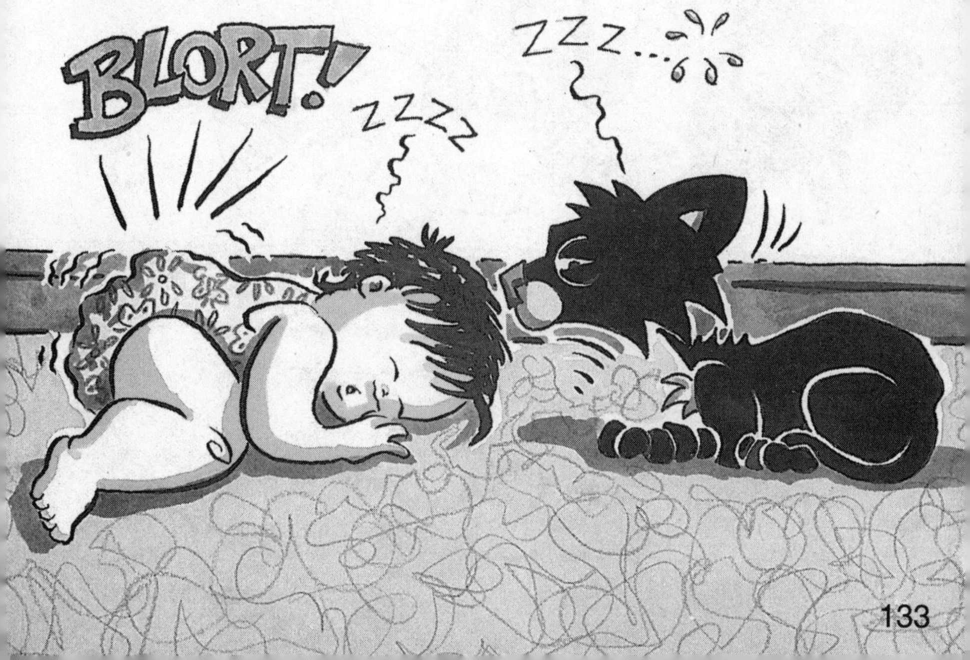

BLORT!
ZZZZ
ZZZ...

No, Kitty! The baby doesn't use the litter box like you.
That's why she wears a diaper.

No, Kitty! The baby doesn't eat cat food like you. That's why we feed her apples and bananas and cereal.

No, Kitty! The baby doesn't play with fuzzy toy mice like you. That's why we give her blocks and cars and teething rings.

No, Kitty! You don't need to lick the baby clean like you clean yourself. That's why we give her a <u>BATH</u>.

That's right, Kitty. Babies get BATHS. Babies like BATHS. In fact, now that this baby is all covered in cat litter, cat food, fuzz, and your slobber, it's time that we gave her a . . .

BATH!

Oh, Kitty. Don't be like that. She likes baths. Really. It's true. Don't you believe me?

What are you doing, Kitty? Are you going to help me take the baby to the bathtub? Are you going to help me give her a bath? Kitty?

Kitty . . . ?

Uh-oh.

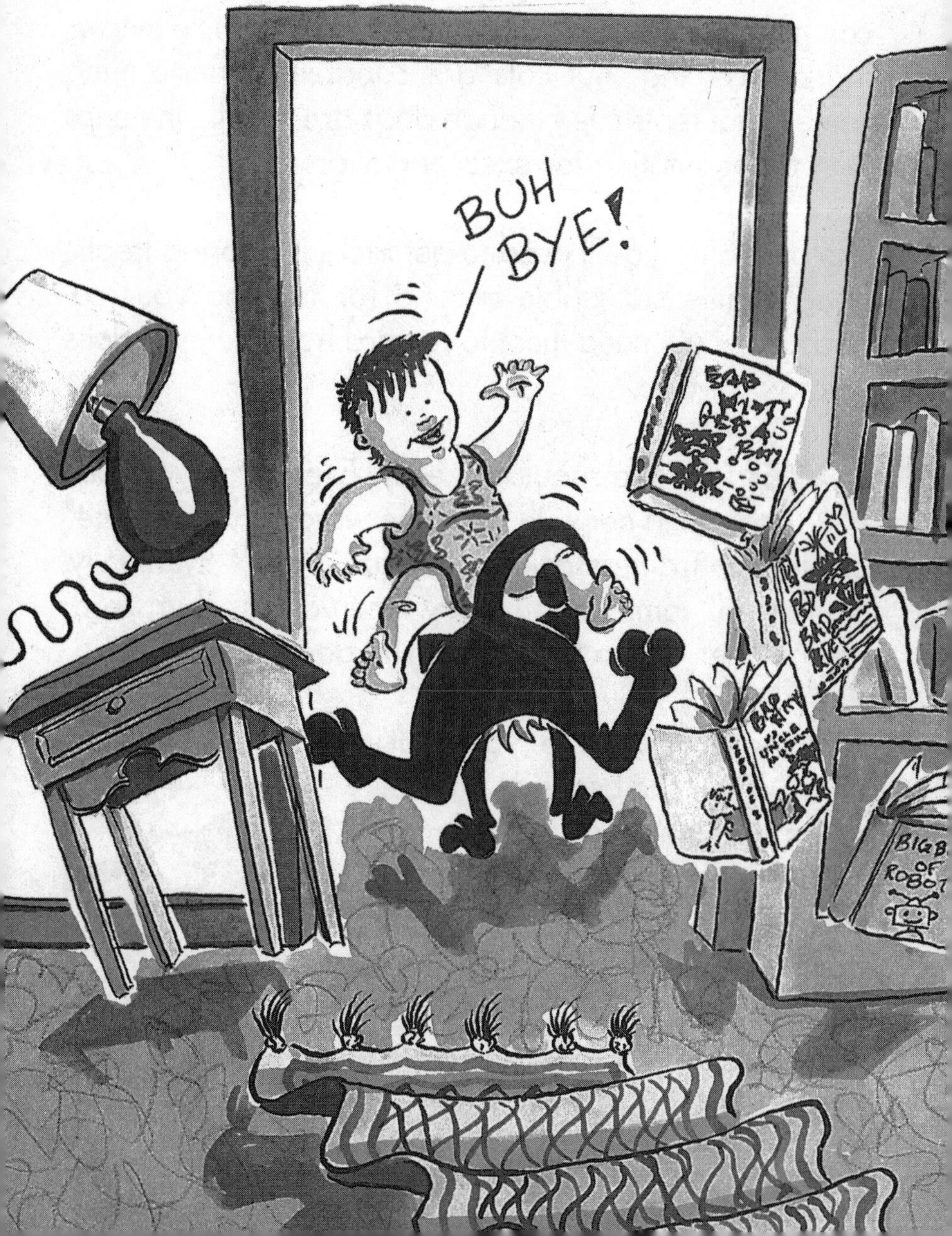
BUH BYE!

• APPENDIX •
CAT TRICKS

During The Pussycat Olympics, we saw all of the kitties compete in some fairly basic feline activities like meowing and eating. But cats are capable of performing some great feats even though dogs are usually the ones with the reputation for executing tricks.

The one thing you'll need to get tricks is to bring treats. Keep a little cat kibble around for training your cat because you'll need them to reward her when she does what you want.

COME: This one should be easy. Every time you feed your cat, call to her with the same word such as "come" or "here." Trainers call this a "cue word." Eventually, the cat will come to you every time you use that word. Reward her with a treat when she does.

SIT: Hold a treat to your cat's nose. When she becomes interested, move the treat up over her head until she naturally takes a sitting position. When she sits down, give her the treat. After you've been able to do this several times, introduce the cue word of "sit" into her training. After a

while, she should be able to sit on command.

SHAKE A PAW: Once you have been able to teach your cat to sit, try gently tapping her front paw while saying "shake." Once she naturally lifts her paw up, gently take it into your hand and then give her a treat.

SITTING UP OR BEGGING: Once your cat has mastered sitting, try holding a treat up a little higher than usual. It will take several tries, but once your cat lifts her front paws off the ground, give her the treat right away. Over time, you can lift the treat higher so the cat has to reach higher. Eventually you may be able to train your cat to sit or even stand up on hind legs alone on command.

When you train your cat, you have to remember two things: BE PATIENT because, depending on the cat, even the simplest tricks can take several days, weeks, or even months to learn. And DON'T OVERFEED YOUR CAT. Tricks are fun to teach your cat, but not at the expense of making her too fat because of all the rewards you're giving her.

TACO, PLEASE!

GOFISH

NICK BRUEL

What did you want to be when you grew up?
I tell this story all the time when I visit schools. When I was in first grade, there was nothing I liked to do more than to write stories and make little drawings to go with them. I thought the best job in the world was the one held by those people who had the comic strips in the newspapers. What better job is there than to wake up each morning and spend the day writing little stories and making little drawings to go along with them. So that's what I did. I wrote stories and I drew pictures to go along with them. And I still do that to this day.

When did you realize you wanted to be a writer?
I always liked to write stories. But it wasn't until high school when I spent a lot of time during summer vacations writing plays for my own amusement that I began to think this was something I could do as a career.

What's your first childhood memory?
Sitting in my high chair feeling outraged that my parents were eating steak and green beans while all I had was a bowl of indescribable mush.

What's your most embarrassing childhood memory?
Crying my eyes out while curled up in my cubbyhole in first grade for reasons I can't remember. I didn't come back out until my mother came in to pick me up from school.

What's your favorite childhood memory?
Waking up early on Christmas morning to see what Santa brought me.

As a young person, who did you look up to most?
My father. He was a kind man with a great sense of humor.

What was your worst subject in school?
True story: In eighth grade, I was on the second string of the B-Team of middle school baseball. I was up at bat only twice the entire season. I struck out and was beaned. It was generally recognized that I was the worst player on the team. And since our team lost every single game it played that year, it was decided that I was probably the worst baseball player in all of New York State in 1978.

What was your best subject in school?
Art, with English coming in a close second.

What was your first job?
I spent most of the summer after my junior year in college as an arts and crafts director at a camp for kids with visual disabilities in Central Florida. I won't say any more, because I'm likely to write a book about it someday.

How did you celebrate publishing your first book?
I honestly don't remember. A lot was happening at that time. When *Boing!* came out, I was also preparing to get married. Plus, I was hard at work on *Bad Kitty*.

Where do you write your books?

As I write this, I'm the father of a one-year-old baby. Because of all the attention she needs, I've developed a recent habit, when the babysitter comes by to watch Isabel, of collecting all of my work together and bringing it to a nice little Chinese restaurant across the street called A Taste of China. They know me pretty well, and let me sit at one of their tables for hours while I nibble on a lunch special.

Where do you find inspiration for your writing?

Other books. The only true axiom to creative expression is that to be productive at what you do, you have to pay attention to what everyone else is doing. I think this is true for writing, for painting, for playing music, for anything that requires any sort of creative output. To put it more simply for my situation . . . if you want to write books, you have to read as many books as you can.

Which of your characters is most like you?

In *Happy Birthday, Bad Kitty*, I introduce a character named Strange Kitty. I can say without any hesitation that Strange Kitty is me as a child. I was definitely the cat who would go to a birthday party and spend the entire time sitting in the corner reading comic books rather than participating in all of the pussycat games.

When you finish a book, who reads it first?

My wife, Carina. Even if I'm on a tight deadline, she'll see it first before I send it to my editor, Neal Porter. Carina has a fine sense of taste for the work I do. I greatly respect her opinion even when she's a little more honest than I'd like her to be.

Are you a morning person or a night owl?
Both. I suspect that I need less sleep than most people. I'm usually the first one up to make breakfast. And I'm rarely in bed before 11:00 PM. Maybe this is why I'm exhausted all the time.

What's your idea of the best meal ever?
So long as it's Chinese food, I don't care. I just love eating it. If I had to pick a favorite dish, it would be Duck Chow Fun, which I can only find in a few seedy diners in Chinatown.

Which do you like better: cats or dogs?
Oh, I know everyone is going to expect me to say cats, but in all honesty, I love them both.

What do you value most in your friends?
Sense of humor and reliability.

Where do you go for peace and quiet?
I'm the father of a one-year-old. What is this "peez kwiet" thing you speak of?

What makes you laugh out loud?
The Marx Brothers. W. C. Fields. Buster Keaton. And my daughter.

What's your favorite song?
I don't think I have one favorite song, but "If You Want to Sing Out, Sing Out" by Cat Stevens comes to mind.

Who is your favorite fictional character?
The original Captain Marvel. He's the kind of superhero designed for kids who need superheroes. SHAZAM!

What are you most afraid of?
Scorpions. ACK! They're like the creepiest parts of spiders and crabs smashed together into one nasty-looking character. Who's idea was that?

What time of year do you like best?
Spring and summer.

What's your favorite TV show?
I have to give my propers to *The Simpsons,* of course. But I'm very partial to the British mystery series *Lovejoy.*

If you were stranded on a desert island, who would you want for company?
I'm going to defy the implications of that question and say no one. As much as I'm comfortable talking for hours with any number of people, I'm also one of those people who relishes solitude. I've never had any problem with being alone for long periods of time. . . . You get a lot more work done that way.

If you could travel in time, where would you go?
America in the 1920s. All of my favorite literature, movies, and music comes from that period. I would love to have witnessed or even participated in the artistic movements of that period in history.

What's the best advice you have ever received about writing?
I had a playwriting teacher in college named Bob Butman who gave me superb advice on the subject of writer's block—it's all about PRIDE. It's a complete myth to believe that you can't think about what you want to write next because your mind is a blank. In truth, when you feel

"blocked," it's because you DO have something in mind that you want to put to paper, but you don't feel it's good enough for what you're trying to accomplish. That's the pride part. The best thing, I find, is to put it down anyways and move on. Half the challenge of the writing process is the self-editing process.

What would you do if you ever stopped writing?
I would seriously consider becoming a teacher.

What do you like best about yourself?
I have nice hands. They've always served me well.

What is your worst habit?
Biting other people's toenails.

What do you consider to be your greatest accomplishment?
Adopting our spectacular daughter, Isabel. Actually managing to get my first book (*Boing!*) published comes in second.

Where in the world do you feel most at home?
Home. I'm a homebody. I like to work at home. I like to cook at home. I like to grow my garden vegetables at home. I like being in new and different places, but I despise the process of getting there. So, because I'm not a big fan of traveling, I just like being at HOME. It's a quality about myself that runs closely with my love of solitude.

What do you wish you could do better?
I wish I was a better artist. I look at the fluidity of line and the luminous colors of paintings by such artists as Ted Lewin, Anik McGrory, Jerry Pinkney, and Arthur Rackham with complete awe.

It's time to elect a new president of the Neighborhood Cat Club. But when one candidate realizes she never registered to vote, the election takes a surprising turn. Will Old Kitty's absentee ballot change everything?

Find out in
Bad Kitty for President

Good morning, Kitty!

Kitty? Kitty?

Wow. Something outside really has your attention today. I wonder what it is. Are there birds? Are there squirrels? Did Brian the mailman drop his lunch again?

Oh, I see. You're looking at some of those stray cats that come wandering in from the neighborhood next to ours every now and then.

What's the big deal, Kitty? They're not hurting any-
one, are they? They're just cats like you.

Well, Kitty, if they're bothering you so much, why don't you do something about it?

I know that look, Kitty. You're thinking about throwing them all into an active volcano, aren't you? *Sigh* That's not what I was talking about.

What I mean is . . . why don't you run for president of the Neighborhood Cat Club? Old Kitty is about to leave office, which means that a new president has to be elected. It might as well be you.

Oh, sure . . . I know that being president is a great responsibility and a lot of hard work. And I know that it requires a lot of personal sacrifice. But maybe you'd do a great job.

And besides, it's the best way I can think of to deal with the stray cat issue in the way that you want most.

That's right, Kitty. As president, you would get to sug-
gest the laws that all of the other kitties would have
to follow, including any law you think would be best
for dealing with the stray cats . . . with the possible
exception of throwing them all into an active volcano.

You see, Kitty, as president you would . . . uh . . .

Where'd she go?

Sorry, Kitty. It's just not that simple. You have to go through a whole lot of very complicated steps before you can become president.